m7

Charlotte Leaves the Light On

ANNETTE SMITH

CENTER POINT PUBLISHING
THORNDIKE, MAINE

This Center Point Large Print edition
is published in the year 2007 by arrangement with
Moody Publishers.

All Scripture quotations are taken from the *Holy Bible,
New International Version*®. NIV®. Copyright © 1973, 1978,
1984 by International Bible Society. Used by permission of
Zondervan Publishing House.

The text of this Large Print edition is unabridged. In other
aspects, this book may vary from the original edition. Printed in
Thailand. Set in 16-point Times New Roman type.

ISBN-10: 1-58547-921-7
ISBN-13: 978-1-58547-921-4

Library of Congress Cataloging-in-Publication Data

Smith, Annette Gail, 1959-
    Charlotte leaves the light on / Annette Smith.--Center Point large print ed.
        p. cm.
    ISBN-13: 978-1-58547-921-4 (lib. bdg. : alk. paper)
        1. Foster mothers--Fiction. 2. Large type books. I. Title.

    PS3619.M55C47 2007
    813'.6--dc22

2006028969

For my daughter-in-love,
Sarah Dean Smith

Acknowledgments

Writing books is the dream-I-never-dared-dream come true. When the UPS man delivers that first case of brand-spanking-new volumes, thank the Lord he's always in a hurry, 'cause it's all I can do not to kiss the man on the lips. There's nothing to compare with the experience of dragging that box into my kitchen, kneeling over it with a butter knife, and slicing through the packing tape to get a first glimpse of my latest book baby.

Many folks, by their influences on my life, have contributed to the joy I've received from the writing and publication of what now comes to an unbelievable ten books. First off, thanks to my husband, Randy, whose eyes always tell me when I've nailed a troublesome scene. It is his sacrificial support that has enabled me to pursue this dream. Waking up next to him is the best part of my day.

My adult children, Rachel and Russell, both make me so proud it's all I can do not to brag about them way, way too much. Russell's new wife, Sarah, has brought happiness to Russell and joy to the rest of us. We're thrilled she's a part of our lives.

Unlike wine, few folks I know of get better with age. My parents, Louie and Marolyn Woodall, are exceptions. They model the selfless spirit of Christ in ways that amaze. Seemingly unaware that they are special in any way, they love the unlovable, serve the undeserving, and give to the ungrateful.

My brother Dayne is my personal computer man, the one who sacrificed three days to put together a bargain machine for me so I could save $200 on a new out-of-the-box model. If he ever gets tired of my calls for techno-help, I'm in big trouble. My brother Bruce is a great encourager and cheerleader, always interested in the details of my latest project. His adventurous, curious spirit inspires me to reach higher and further.

Among a host of fun folks I call my friends, I'm blessed to have a dear handful who "get" what I do. I thank Jeanna Lambert, Susan Duke, Sheri Harrison, Sheila Cook, and Laura Walker. My life's course was changed by the enthusiastic support of my former agent, now friend, Chip Macgregor. For him I am grateful. The unselfish spirit of best-selling author Debra White Smith, evidenced by generous, timely, professional advice, still humbles me. She helped make this book what it is.

I so appreciate the good folks at Moody for putting Ruby Prairie on the map. Special thanks to Andy McGuire and Lori Wenzinger for the confidence they place in me. Thanks also to editor LB Norton, who slices and dices so cleanly one hardly feels the pain.

And special thanks to you, dear reader, for joining me on this journey to the town of my dreams.

To God be the glory

Annette loves to hear from her readers.
Contact her at P.O. Box 835, Quitman, TX 75783
or via her Web site, www.annettesmithbooks.com

Chapter One

Sugar.
  Water.
Cranberries.

In the overheated kitchen of Tanglewood, Charlotte Carter pushed a damp, strawberry blonde curl back with her forearm, then swirled the mixture in her jumbo-sized pot with a long wooden spoon. She stirred clockwise for a while. Then changed to counterclockwise. No matter how she coaxed with her spoon, the cranberries, four bags of them, floated to the top of the watery solution.

Charlotte plucked her reading glasses from the pocket of her floral print overalls. Cranberry sauce was supposed to be, um, saucy. Not soupy. She set the spoon on the counter, then began digging in the trash can under the sink for one of the tossed-out cranberry bags.

At forty-two, Charlotte had no problem admitting to being a less-than-expert cook. Until this very afternoon she had never attempted cranberry sauce. Surely you were supposed to add something else—an ingredient to make the stuff thicken up.

Flour?

Cornstarch, maybe?

Not according to the directions on the bag.

She gave the mixture another optimistic swirl. Berries bobbed to the surface like persistent plastic fishing floats. Making a simple sauce should not be this much of a challenge. She stirred some more.

Cranberry sauce was Charlotte's assigned contribution to the Ruby Prairie community Thanksgiving meal. It was her church's turn to serve as the host congregation. She had to come through. For Lighted Way. For the community.

For Jock?

Whatever you do, work at it with all your heart, as working for the Lord, not for men. . . .

Through the small-town grapevine, Charlotte knew it was to the delight of Ruby Prairie matchmakers that she and Pastor Jock Masters had been out on three dates. Three dates in four months, according to those in the know.

Less than a week ago Kerilynn Bell, Ruby Prairie's first female mayor and longtime owner of the 'Round the Clock Café, had plopped her skinny behind down in Tanglewood's cozy kitchen for no other purpose other than to quiz Charlotte about what exactly was taking her and Jock so long to get this relationship off the ground.

"No offense, sugar," Kerilynn said, "but you and Pastor are neither one spring chickens. Y'all are meandering along like you've got all the time in the world. Time's passing you by."

"Thanks for pointing that out," Charlotte said. "Perhaps I should look into booking a room out at New Energy. I hear the food's good and they have bingo twice a week."

Kerilynn let the comment slide. "You two are perfect for each other. Single. Attractive. Intelligent. Near the same age."

"Still have our own teeth . . ."

"Terrible waste, not taking advantage of the situation and getting together."

"We are together," said Charlotte. "We're friends. Busy friends. No time for more than that." She got up to refill Kerilynn's coffee cup.

The truth? Charlotte supposed neither she nor Jock knew exactly how to go about this sort of thing. Were they attracted to each other? It seemed so—though they had never so much as shared a kiss.

Most of Ruby Prairie's two thousand citizens knew at least something about Charlotte's story. After losing J.D., her husband of twenty years, she'd moved to Texas and bought Tanglewood, now home to her and a houseful of troubled young girls.

In a late-night talk out on Tanglewood's wraparound porch, Jock had haltingly shared with her painful bits of his more private, troubled past. His story included a young, hasty marriage, infidelity—his, he acknowledged—the miscarriage of their child, followed by a quick divorce. Even though he knew God had forgiven him every wrong he'd ever done, the memories were still painful.

They both hauled parts of their pasts around with

them like heavy, overstuffed bags. She, tender memories and grief. He, lingering remorse, guilt, and the unshakable fear of inflicting hurt again.

Charlotte glanced at her watch and peered out the window at a hard-falling rain. Three o'clock. In ten minutes she'd need to leave for school to pick up the girls. They shouldn't walk home on a nasty day like this. Could she leave the sauce and come back to it, or was it like a cake, where once you got it started, you had to see it through?

She turned from the pot on the stove to phone Ginger Collins next door, one of Ruby Prairie's most sensible cooks. Shifting her weight from one white-socked foot to the other, Charlotte twirled the phone cord around her slim wrist.

"Sorry to bother you, Ginger. I'm making the cranberry sauce for tomorrow night's dinner, and something's not right."

"Oh, honey," Ginger said, "you didn't have to go to the trouble of cooking all that up. Canned from Rick's Grocery would do fine."

Charlotte picked at the cuticle of a nail-bitten hand. "I was going do just that, but Kerilynn said everybody likes the whole berry kind. All Rick's had was jellied. Nomie was in the store, and she said cooking it from scratch was easy. But I must have done something wrong."

"Nomie's right. Nothing to it. Just a little sugar and water. You probably don't have your fire up hot enough. Honey, I'll come right over, but you've got to

14

be patient. Keep stirring. Let your sauce come to a slow boil."

Pop. Pop.

POP!

Charlotte turned back to the stove. "Ginger, is it supposed to—?"

As if on cue, hot cranberries began exploding wildly, sending airborne spurts of fuchsia goo all over the stove. Charlotte stood frozen to the floor as the boiling mass rose higher and higher until it began cascading over the sides of the pot like flowing lava. Acrid, burned-sugar smoke rose from the red-hot burner, setting off the kitchen smoke detector.

"Oh, my!" said Charlotte. "Ginger, I've gotta go."

Chapter Two

Jock Masters, working in his windowless, pine-paneled pastor's office at the church, tried to talk himself out of a snack. He got up from his desk, stretched, looked at his watch, sucked in his forty-one-year-old stomach, and sat back down.

Four thirty. Five hours since lunch. Two hours till dinner.

He should wait.

Mornings and early afternoons were always hectic. Lighted Way Church had no secretary, so Jock fielded phone calls and put together the weekly bulletin. He provided counsel and prayer to members in need and made visits and calls to the sick and shut-in. But few folks stopped by or even called after three. By four, four thirty, people all over town were winding down their days, returning to their families and homes—which was why he reserved the quiet of his late afternoons for prayer and study.

The sermon for tomorrow night's Thanksgiving eve service needed more work. Jock picked up a yellow highlighter, fiddled with it a bit, then laid it down to thumb through the day's mail—for the second time in an hour.

His stomach growled.

The spirit was willing.

The flesh weak.

Dinner?

Baked chicken probably. Rice-a-Roni. Salad. He was trying to eat more vegetables. Too bad creamed corn didn't count.

His stomach growled again. Alice Buck had delivered a batch of her oatmeal apple butter bars to the office this morning. His favorite. To decrease the duration of the treat's torment, he'd shared them with the Tuesday noontime prayer group, offered them seconds, then nagged them all to take thirds. But his mouth watered at the thought of the last two remaining cookies wrapped in foil, sitting next to the coffeepot in the church kitchen.

Calling his name.

Jock was six feet tall and carried his extra ten pounds well. As long as the ten didn't turn into twenty, he figured he was okay. But serving a congregation of some of east Texas's finest bakers did not help his dieting efforts one bit. By the frequency of their offerings, Jock wondered if a few of the good cooks thought bringing him samples of their best could nudge them closer to the pearly gates.

The bones of the sixty-year-old church building groaned and creaked. Then Jock heard the pounding of drops of rain on the roof. As predicted, a thunderstorm was blowing through. He shivered. Like a polar bear preparing to hibernate, he couldn't shake the desire to snack.

Hot chocolate.

Low fat, of course.

From the top of his desk, Jock scooped up his key ring and put on his coat. He whistled as he strode down the narrow hallway toward the back door.

Of the two structures that Lighted Way comprised, the main building, where Jock had his office, was fashioned in a southern Protestant style common in the 1940s. Little had been changed in the years since its construction.

Worshipers who came in the front entered a closet-sized foyer furnished with a tract rack and a water fountain. Years ago, someone had equipped the fountain with a set of homemade wooden steps for small children. On either side of the foyer were the restrooms—men's on the right, women's on the left.

Through swinging double doors people entered the sanctuary. Pairs of oak pews, with padding added in the seventies, parted to form a center aisle that led to the elevated pulpit. Behind the lectern was the baptistery (Lighted Way immersed) framed by purple velvet curtains, with artificial ivy in front. There was no altar; rather, a simple communion table stood covered with a crocheted cloth. High on the wall, over the baptistery, hung a six-foot wooden cross. Classrooms and Jock's office were located on either side of the sanctuary, reached through long, narrow halls.

Though built to hold one hundred and fifty worshipers, most Sundays Jock preached to eighty-five or ninety faithful Lighted Way folks. When he'd first arrived six years before, attendance had hovered around sixty. While not exactly phenomenal growth, every year the church had inched a bit in the right direction.

Unlike the attractive, steepled white sanctuary, the fellowship hall and kitchen were housed in a utilitarian, rectangular, tan metal structure. Thanks to budget-minded deacons, the building had been designed with economy and function in mind, rather than beauty. Inside, the space was much the no-nonsense same. Tile floor. Long tables. Folding chairs. Kitchen on the far end, restrooms on the near. Though he was thankful for the hall, which was put to good use almost every day of the week, Jock was glad that it was tucked behind the main building, barely visible from the street.

The two separate structures were connected to each other by a covered drive-through made for convenient back-door pickups and drop-offs in bad weather. It never failed to touch Jock's heart to observe young men letting their wives and children out under the covered shelter, parking their own vehicles, then sprinting waterlogged back through the rain, only to do it all over again and again, providing valet parking for church widows who shouldn't get wet.

Since the parsonage was located across the street from the church, Jock usually walked to work. However, since early afternoon his truck had been parked under the awning, where he'd left it after unloading paper goods purchased for tomorrow's meal. Good thing. When he was done for the day he could drive himself home instead of having to sprint across the street in the rain.

Jock crossed quickly from the sanctuary to the fellowship hall. He fumbled for the right key, then realized the building had been left open, most likely by the last straggler of the noontime prayer group.

What weather. Rain was now coming down in sheets. It misted Jock's face, wet his short, gray-flecked beard, and plastered his brown curls to the back of his neck. He stepped inside and felt for the light. The fluorescents flickered, then blinked, then finally came on—but not for long. Jock was halfway to the kitchen when a booming clap of thunder shook the panes of the windows, and the lights went out.

Thunderstorm power outages happened frequently

in Ruby Prairie. Mayor Kerilynn said it was because of all the trees. From past experience, he knew it might be hours before the electricity returned—which meant Jock was going home.

He whistled as he felt along a wall toward the kitchen, intent now upon snagging the leftover cookies. As for supper, didn't he have a couple of cans of chili at home? Forget baked chicken. This was chili weather. Fritos. Chopped onions. Grated cheese. Tall glass of sweet iced tea. Calling it a day and leaving his office a bit early was sounding better all the time. Yes. Ten minutes from now he would be home in front of a fire, burrowed in for the night.

He was reaching for the foil-wrapped paper plate when he heard a sound. Not exactly a sound, rather a movement. Soft rustling. From somewhere down low.

He stopped whistling. "Hello?"

No answer, just the feeling that *something* was there.

"Can I help you?"

Jock waited. Must have been the wind, or a tree branch brushing up against an outside wall.

His eyes had adjusted enough in the darkness that he could make his way back to the door.

There it was again. He was not alone. Jock's heart pounded. What he'd heard wasn't even a sound exactly—it was more like a feeling, an unmistakable awareness that someone, *something* else was in the room.

He fought the urge to bolt.

Lord, help me.

20

He'd eased two steps toward the outside door when the lights suddenly flickered back on. He turned around. When his eyes found the unexpected source of the odd sounds, Jock drew a quick breath and fumbled for his cell phone. He held it in his sweaty hand, trying to decide what numbers to punch. 9-1-1, he guessed. But what exactly was it he needed?

The police?

An ambulancc?

No. Charlotte. She would know what to do.

The connection was weak.

"Who is this?" Charlotte was sitting cross-legged on the floor in front of the fire, playing Crazy Eights with the ten-year-old Tanglewood twins, Nikki and Vikki. It was her turn to go.

"It's Jock."

"Who?" Probably some telemarketer trying to sell siding or calling to tell her she'd won a free cruise.

"Nikki—it's your go," she said with her hand over the phone. Then, "Who wants to play the next game? I've got to fix us some supper."

Maggie and Sharita were finishing up their homework at the kitchen table. Donna was curled up on one of the room's overstuffed, ticking-striped sofas, reading a book.

"I do!" said Sharita.

"What're we having?" asked Donna.

"Charlotte, it's Jock. I'm at the church. Could you come down here? To the fellowship hall?"

"Jock?" Charlotte looked out the window to see lightning and torrents of rain. "I'm sorry. What'd you say?"

"I said I need you to come down here. If you can. To the church."

"Now?" She laid down her hand of cards.

"I've got a situation here, and I'm not sure what to do." Jock's usually calm voice sounded strained.

A situation?

"Well, sure. I'll be happy to come down, but would it be all right if I wait until the rain lets up a bit? I hate to leave the girls thinking that the lights might go off. Sharita and Donna are both a little spooky when it comes to storms."

"I'm *real* spooky," called Sharita from the table. "One time my cousin got her house blown all the way down. She was in the bathtub when it happened, and she was naked too."

Donna rolled her eyes.

On the other end of the phone, Jock was silent for a long moment. Finally he spoke. "Sure. Okay."

"You'll still be at the church?" asked Charlotte. She didn't want to be rude, but did he realize what time it was?

"I'll be here."

"Okeydokey. Be down there soon as it lets up." Charlotte hung up the phone.

"Who was that?" asked Vikki.

"Pastor Jock."

"What'd he want?" asked Nikki.

22

"Needs some help at the church. Probably with the setup for tomorrow night's dinner," said Charlotte.

"You gone tell him 'bout how you messed up all those cranberries?" asked Sharita, fingering one of her droopy dreadlocks.

"No, I'm not going to tell him," said Charlotte.

Forget homemade cranberry sauce. Ginger was right. Canned would be fine.

"And neither are any of you!" She grinned. It had taken her and Ginger forever to get the sticky mess cleaned up. Her sauce-making days were done.

"We're gon-na te-ell. We're gon-na te-ell," Maggie and Sharita sang.

Charlotte made the girls an early supper of grilled cheese sandwiches and chicken noodle soup. Donna set the table without being asked.

While Maggie and Nikki had seconds, Charlotte stepped out onto the porch to stare up at the sky. A gust of wind stirred stray piles of leaves. She shivered, wishing she hadn't told Jock she would come.

Maybe he'd changed his mind about whatever it was he thought needed doing. Perhaps he'd given up and gone home himself.

She went inside and dialed his number just to check. It rang ten times.

Charlotte pulled her van into the church parking lot.

Great. Just great.

Jock's truck was parked square in the middle of the covered walkway, which meant she'd have to park her van out in the rain and make a dash for it. In her hurry to leave, she'd forgotten her umbrella—though lots of good it would have done in this wind. Again she wondered what was so important that it couldn't wait until tomorrow.

Lord, give me the heart of a servant, Charlotte prayed as she ran for cover. *Forgive me my attitude. Help me to love as You love, serve as You serve.*

"Jock?" She pushed the heavy door open. "I'm here. What is it you need me to—"

Sitting on a folding chair in the kitchen, holding some kind of a bundle, Jock looked up when he heard Charlotte come in. Blood had run down his temple and dried on his cheek.

"Jock! What happened? Are you all right?" She dropped her purse and rushed toward him.

"I—I found something," he said when she was at his side. "I wasn't sure who I should call."

"What are you talking about?"

He wasn't making any sense—and he did in fact have a big gash just above his left eye.

"Did you fall?" Guilt swept over her. "I'm sorry I didn't come when you first called. We better get this cleaned up. You may need stitches."

"Charlotte." Jock's voice was even. "I'm fine. But look." He moved to show her what he was holding. "I—I don't know what to do."

Charlotte looked.

At a *baby.*

In Jock's arms.

A clap of thunder made them both jump. Then the lights went out.

Wearing a red apron with the words Kiss the Cook screen-printed across the bosom, Treasure Jones stood at the sink in her farmhouse kitchen. She was washing a bunch of gritty fall turnip greens, checking the dark leaves carefully to make sure a worm didn't accidentally get cooked up in the pot.

Since she and Jasper had eloped six months earlier, Treasure's evenings had evolved into a routine. There were always adjustments in marriage. One she'd had to make was the preparing and eating of supper late in the day. The evening care and feeding of the dozen horses her handsome husband kept on the place always came first, a fact she understood and accepted.

The steeds earned their keep. Four afternoons a week, Jasper gave riding lessons to supplement his monthly teacher retirement check. Treasure was proud of her husband's glowing reputation. Word had spread that he was a kind, insightful instructor who had a way with jumpy horses and their nervous new riders. Some of Jasper's students traveled as far as fifty miles for their lessons.

Their land and low-slung home, located just outside the Ruby Prairie city limits, was the perfect setting for such a business. The white house with black shutters and a cherry-red front door, surrounded by trees and a tidy board fence, was one of the most inviting and friendly looking places Treasure had ever laid eyes on.

When, after her second riding lesson, Jasper had invited her in for coffee, she'd seen that the inside of the house was as warm and comfortable as the outside.

It was a simple place, three bedrooms down a family-photo-lined center hall, two baths, a large eat-in kitchen, a living room, and a mudroom—plenty of space for the two of them. Treasure especially loved the front porch that ran the length of the ranch-style house. For their one-month anniversary, Jasper had surprised her by hanging a comfortable porch swing. Almost every morning she had her coffee while sitting outside.

But the newlyweds, Jasper an early retired fifty-five, she an energetic sixty-two, did not have much privacy. Only days after their marriage, they'd taken in the shaggy-haired, sad-eyed Kirby, sixteen years old, unwanted and unloved. There had been some rough patches, but all in all, taking in Kirby had been a good thing. God's hand was upon them all was what Treasure truly believed.

She put the greens on to boil and remembered she needed to brew tea.

Treasure had wondered at first if it would be an adjustment for Kirby—a white teenager living with a middle-aged African American couple in a pretty much white Texas town. And could he adapt to the country-style soul food she and Jasper preferred?

Obviously, her worry on that count had been for naught. Kirby gobbled smothered chicken, fried pork chops, greens, okra, corn bread, sweet potato pie, and peach cobbler as though he had eaten such food all his life. He told Treasure over and over what an incredible cook she was. Until coming to live with her, he said, he thought all food came out of some kind of a box or a bag.

"Homework?" Jasper asked after he and Kirby had finished the supper dishes.

"World geography. Got to read a chapter and fill out some worksheet." Kirby found his backpack and hefted it onto the kitchen table.

Jasper elevated the foot of his recliner. "How long's your chapter, son?"

"Not too long. But I can't find my pen. Do you have one?"

"Second drawer under the microwave," said Treasure.

The phone rang, and Kirby jumped up to answer, then handed it to Treasure.

It was Charlotte on the other end of the line. She was breathing hard.

"Are you all right?" Treasure could almost read her best friend's mind. "Something wrong with one of the girls?"

"I'm okay. But I need a little help. I know it's late, but—"

It was all she had to say.

"You need me at the house? Honey, I'm coming. Just give me time to put on my shoes."

Chapter Three

Lights were out all over Ruby Prairie. Treasure, Jasper, and Kirby passed two parked utility trucks on their way into town. The rain was still coming down hard, and the windshield wipers on Jasper's Dooley pickup thumped back and forth rhythmically, swishing sheets of water with every swipe. So loud was the pelting of raindrops on the roof of the truck, Jasper had given up trying to hear the radio weather report. The transmission was mostly static anyway.

"Y'all did not have to come with me," said Treasure for the third time. After living as an independent divorced woman for thirty years, she was not accustomed to being looked after by a man—even a kind, good-looking one like her new husband.

"Honey, we're in a flash flood watch," said Jasper. "That van of yours doesn't sit up near as high as you think it does. All it'd take for you to get stranded would be for you to come upon a low place in the road and stall out. Nobody should be out by themselves in this mess."

"I don't know how long I'll be." Treasure looked at her watch. "Charlotte was in such a hurry to get off the phone, she didn't tell me where she was or how long she'd be gone. I cannot imagine what possessed her to

28

go anywhere in weather like this."

"How come we had lights at our house, but nobody does in town?" asked Kirby from the backseat.

"We're on a different line," said Jasper. He steered slowly into town.

Unlike many small Texas towns, Ruby Prairie did not have a square; there was just a main, through-the-center-of-town street. The majority of businesses lined both sides. Jasper crept along. Only New Energy Rest Home, near the edge of town close to the interstate, was illuminated, but more dimly than usual.

"Must have emergency generators," said Jasper. Across the street from New Energy, Dr. Lee Ross's Four Paws Pet Clinic was completely dark. So were Hometown Tire and Implement, Lighted Way Church, and the Ruby Prairie school.

"Bless those poor folks' hearts," said Treasure, of the residents in the rest home. "I bet storms get the best of them all shook up. So many of them poor souls on oxygen."

They passed Lila's Beauty Shop, Hardy's Hardware, the 'Round-the-Clock Café, then the Chamber of Commerce, Field of Dreams Florist, Joe's Italian Eatery, and Grandma Had One, Ruby Prairie's antique mall. Even though it was barely past seven o'clock, the street was mostly deserted. Even the streetlights and the town's one stoplight were dark.

"Kind of creepy," said Kirby. "Wonder if they'll cancel school tomorrow."

Jasper grinned at Kirby in his rearview mirror.

"Wouldn't count on it, son. They'll have things up and running well before morning, be my guess."

"Hope so. This could be bad for Rick at the grocery store," said Treasure.

"Be bad for everybody if the power stays off long," said Jasper.

Main Street, which began at the north end of Ruby Prairie out near the interstate, ended directly at Tanglewood's picket fence gate. The mailing address was 411 Betty Drive, though locals just directed seekers to "the big pink house at the far end of Main."

So as to not block the driveway, Jasper parked his truck on the street in front. The three of them made their way through the gate, up the sidewalk, and onto the wraparound porch.

"Wipe your feet," said Treasure. The wind whipped at her legs as she tried to turn the knob on the front door. "Lands. Those girls have got it locked up tight." She rang the bell.

Kirby and Jasper, noses to the glass, tried to peer inside the floor-to-ceiling, lace-curtained windows framing each side of the ornately carved door.

"Somebody's coming," said Kirby.

"Looks like three flashlights," said Jasper.

"Girls, it's me. Treasure. Open up."

Giggles and whispers were heard from inside. Then there was a back-and-forth fumbling of the lock. Finally the knob turned.

Treasure pushed the door open. " 'Bout time y'all decided to let me in," she teased.

Five wide-eyed females, all under the age of sixteen, stood in a tight wad in the dark, tall-ceilinged entryway.

"Man! Are we glad to see you," said Maggie, shining her flashlight in Treasure's face.

Treasure shielded her eyes. "I'm glad to see you too, but I'm blind with you all a-shining them lights in my face." She scooped the five of them up into a group hug. "Y'all all right?"

"Charlotte had to go to the church," said Sharita.

"Right after she left, the lights went out," said Donna.

"And we got scared," said the twins in near unison.

"Now, now." Treasure clucked her tongue. "Just a little rain. Nothing to be scared about."

"But it's dark," said Nikki, who was still in Treasure's arms. "And there's thunder and lightning."

"I ain't scared of the dark," bragged Maggie with a toss of her red hair.

"Then why come were you the only one crying like a little baby when the lights went out?" said Sharita.

"Shut up," said Maggie.

"You aren't supposed to say that," said Vikki.

"Say what?" said Maggie.

"Shut up."

"Then how come you just said it?" asked Maggie.

"But—"

Out on the porch, Jasper coughed.

"Enough. Both of you," said Treasure. "Ever'body decent? Jasper, Kirby, it's clear. Y'all can come on in."

31

"Evening, ladies," said Jasper. He and Kirby stepped inside.

Maggie frogged Kirby on the arm. "Hey. What are you doing here?"

"Hi, Mr. Jones," said Donna.

"Sure is dark in here," said Jasper.

"Charlotte told us not to light any candles while she was gone," said Donna.

"That was smart," said Treasure. "But now we're here, let's see if we can find us some. Believe there's a bunch in one of those kitchen drawers. Darlin', let me have your flashlight."

She made her way through the living room, then groped her way past the big round oak table in the breakfast room to the kitchen.

"See," she said, coming back into the living room with a pair of lit tapers, "it's not so bad in here."

Jasper eyed the dark living room hearth. "I say we need to get us a fire lit. Kirby, bring in some wood from the porch, would you, son?"

"Yes, sir."

"I'll help you," said Sharita.

"Not without putting on your shoes," said Treasure. She moved the fireplace screen. "I can't imagine what business in the world Charlotte had over at Lighted Way," she said to no one in particular. "Lights are out all over town. Can't be any power there either."

"I hate storms." Sharita flopped down on the sofa, disturbing Visa and Snowball. The cats scampered to the safety of Charlotte's downstairs bedroom.

"I'm hungry," said Maggie.

"I wish Charlotte would get back," said Donna.

"How long's she been gone, sugar?" asked Jasper.

"Not very long. Pastor Jock called her and asked her to come down to the church. When the lights went out, she called us and said she couldn't come home yet, but she'd call you to come stay with us."

Treasure looked around at the five anxious faces. She'd lived at Tanglewood for half a year before marrying Jasper, helping Charlotte care for this brood, and she loved every one of them. But, lands, they were an emotional bunch. Got worked up about little things. And who could blame them? Charlotte, though she loved and cared for them as her own, wasn't their mother, and Tanglewood wasn't their permanent home.

Donna's mother had left when she was a baby. Last fall her daddy had impulsively taken an offshore drilling job, leaving his daughter with no place to go, no one to care for her. Donna lived for the day when he would come home and they could be together again.

Prior to coming to Tanglewood, Nikki and Vikki had lived with their mother and grandmother. When their mother got cancer, the load of caring for both her ill daughter and her two granddaughters had been too much for their grandmother. But the twins' mother was doing better, and it was likely that they would return home within a few months.

Sharita was the only one who came from an intact,

two-parent home. Her folks were hardworking people who lived in a gang-infested neighborhood. After their son was killed in a drive-by shooting, they had placed Sharita at Tanglewood to keep her safe.

And Maggie? Well, that girl was a hoot, the one to make you want to laugh and pull your hair out all at the same time. She'd come to Tanglewood when rangers found her and her mother, who was wanted by the police for writing hot checks, living in a van at a state park.

There had been a sixth girl at Tanglewood, Beth. Since she left for boarding school in Colorado, Treasure knew that social worker Kim Beeson had been pressing Charlotte as to when she'd be ready to take another girl.

"Kirby," said Nikki, interrupting Treasure's reverie, "wanna play Uno?"

"Sure," he said.

"That's a stupid game," said Maggie.

Treasure shot her a look.

"You wanna play?" asked Vikki. She and Nikki and Kirby sat cross-legged in front of the hearth.

"I guess so. Nothing else to do," said Maggie.

"I'm hungry," said Sharita.

"Didn't you have supper?" asked Treasure.

"Just some soup."

"Seeing as how Charlotte's stove is electric, there's not much way I can do any cooking," said Treasure.

"You could use the microwave," said Nikki.

"Well, duh," said Maggie. "It has to have electricity too."

"I didn't know." Nikki chewed on a fingernail.

"Y'all got any marshmallows?" asked Jasper. His fire had caught, and the orange flames illuminated their faces and cast giant, pantomime-like shadows of the threesome on the opposite high-ceilinged wall.

"Yeah!" said Sharita. "We can roast marshmallows in the fireplace. Me first!"

"I'm not very hungry," said Donna.

Treasure saw her look at her watch for about the fifth time since they had arrived.

"I wish Charlotte was home." Her chin trembled. "Do you think she's okay?"

Chapter Four

Charlotte gazed at the infant wrapped in a ragged blue bath towel.

"What?" she began.

"Who?" she said.

"When?" she whispered, dropping to her knees beside Jock's folding chair.

"I don't know," said Jock. "I don't know anything." He shifted a bit in his chair, careful not to jostle the dozing baby, who stirred and made little sucking sounds in his sleep.

"Where did he come from?" Charlotte finally got her words out. "Whose is he?"

"I don't know," said Jock. "I was working in my office. Came over to get some hot chocolate and found the door unlocked. When I got inside, there he was. Under that table."

"On the floor?"

Jock nodded.

"I can't believe someone would do this," said Charlotte. "Was there a note?"

"No. Nothing." Jock touched the lump near his temple.

"What happened to your head?"

"Bumped my head on the corner of the table when I was down on all fours."

"Jock, this is crazy. We have to call someone," said Charlotte.

"I know, but who?"

"I think we have to take him to a hospital. He's so tiny. I wonder how old he is."

"If he's abandoned, the police have to be contacted," said Jock.

"What will they do?" asked Charlotte.

"Don't know. I doubt Mark down at the station has had much experience with abandoned babies."

"How about I call Kim Beeson?" said Charlotte. "You know. The girls' social worker. Maybe she can tell us what to do. Then we'll call Mark."

The baby stirred and blinked in Jock's arms. Silently, in the stillness of the candlelit room, Jock and Charlotte gazed into the infant's soulful, damp eyes. His tiny hand escaped the ragged wrappings.

36

Jock placed his index finger in the little creased palm, and the baby instantly held on. "Look at that," Jock breathed. "Look at that."

"He's beautiful," said Charlotte finally. Unbidden, thoughts of her struggle with infertility, thoughts buried in a shallow grave in her heart, rose up to choke her voice. "How could anyone—?"

Teenagers in the news could get pregnant in the backseats of cars, eat potato chips and drink Coke for nine months, receive no prenatal care, and still manage to deliver healthy bouncing babies. Adult friends and coworkers could get pregnant for the third and fourth times while using birth control. But despite a plethora of tests, pills and shots, and an array of embarrassing and painful procedures, only once in their twenty-year marriage had she and J.D. accomplished a pregnancy. They'd been ecstatic—for three weeks—then devastated by the miscarriage that followed. During those years, she would have given *any-thing*—anything to hold an infant that was hers, theirs, in her arms.

She could not take her eyes off this beautiful boy.

The storm passed over Ruby Prairie, and lights came back on all over town. Kirby and the Tanglewood girls, full of marshmallows, popcorn, and hot chocolate, sprawled in the living room watching a DVD.

Treasure and Jasper sat at Charlotte's round oak dining table sipping coffee. Out of earshot of the girls they spoke in low tones.

"Not like Charlotte not to call," said Treasure.

"You reckon the phone lines are down?"

"They're not. I checked. Besides, she's got a cell."

"Something's not right," said Jasper. "You call the church?"

"No answer." Treasure turned her attention to the girls. "What're y'all watching in there?" she called.

"*Iron Will*," said Donna. "It's about a sled race."

"I've seen that show. Good one," said Jasper.

"I had a dog like that one time," Maggie said of the sled dogs on the screen. "Except for he was black."

Nikki and Vikki each held a sleeping dog in her lap. "You want to be in a race, Mavis?" asked Nikki.

"Do they let cats race?" asked Sharita. Snowball and Visa, two balls of white fur, were curled up on the warm hearth.

"Shhh," said Maggie. "This is the good part."

Jasper drained his mug, then got up to fetch more wood for the fire. "Treasure," he called before opening up the front door. "Can you come here a second?"

Treasure picked her way through the living room toward the adjacent entry hall, doing her best to avoid stepping on any of the human, feline, or canine bodies cozied up to the fire and the TV.

Jasper pushed aside the lace curtain and peered out the window. "Look here," he said.

Treasure saw a line of car headlights snaking its way up Main, heading straight toward Tanglewood.

"What's going on?" asked Donna.

"I wanna see," said Maggie.

"Hit pause," said Kirby.

The five girls and Kirby clambered to see out the window on the other side of the door.

"All y'all," said Treasure, "go back to your movie. Let me and Jasper see what it is that's going on."

Not one of them moved. Shivering in stocking feet on the cold floor, they watched as car after car either parked on the street in front of Tanglewood or pulled into the driveway.

"Who is it?" asked Donna, at the back of the pack.

"What's all those cars doing coming here?" asked Maggie.

The dogs began to bark.

The cats ran to hide under Charlotte's bed.

Jasper opened the front door as Nomie Jenkins and Alice Buck, each carrying a bulky cardboard box, stepped onto the porch. Coming up the walk on their heels was Kerilynn Bell, followed by her brother, Catfish Martin. They also carried boxes, along with a big black plastic garbage sack. From around the side of the house came Lester and Ginger Collins. He was toting some kind of a wooden frame, she two large shopping bags. Out front he could see Lila Peterson and her two little girls, and at least half a dozen other folks coming along behind.

"What in the world," said Treasure. "Donna, you and Maggie get those dogs out of here so Ginger can come inside. You know how scared she is of them. Sharita, what are you doing? Get yourself back into this house. You'll catch cold out on that porch without any shoes."

"We heard," said Nomie. She wiped her feet on the welcome mat.

"Lands," said Catfish. He pushed his way inside.

"I never heard of such," said Alice.

"Not in Ruby Prairie," finished Lester Collins, breathing hard from the load he was carrying.

Ginger made sure the coast was clear before she, too, stepped in. "Where you want us to set this up, sugar?"

"Set what up? What are y'all talking about?" Treasure was stunned at the unexpected crowd tracking up the shiny wood floor of Tanglewood's entryway. "What is all this? And do any of you know where Charlotte is?"

"You don't know?" asked Kerilynn.

"Know what?"

"I heard it on my scanner," explained Catfish.

"He called me," said Lester.

"Then I called everyone else," said Ginger.

Jasper raised his voice. "Has there been an accident?"

"Is Charlotte all right?" asked Treasure at the same time.

Donna tuned up to cry. Nikki and Vikki, wide-eyed and all ears, plastered themselves to either side of Treasure.

"Jock found an abandoned little baby in the fellowship hall down at the church," said Kerilynn.

"According to what Catfish heard Mark say on his police radio, once they get the little thing checked out by the doctor, Charlotte'll be bringing it here. In all the county, Tanglewood's the only foster home that has a space."

"Which is why we're here," explained Ginger. "Lester and me brought over the portable crib we keep on hand for the grandkids."

"I brought blankets and crib sheets," said Lila Peterson. "I've never gotten rid of them, even though it's been years since my girls were small enough for a baby bed."

"The Culture Club keeps things on hand in our emergency closet for families in need. I went down and got the baby some diapers and wipes for his little bottom," said Nomie, who was president.

"Food pantry at First Baptist keeps baby formula. Pete Perry's my neighbor and he's a deacon down there," said Chilly Reed. "Which in my opinion is something we ought to be doing down at Lighted Way. Anyway, he let me take as much of their baby milk as I wanted. Since I didn't know what kind the little one would need, I got a case of every brand they had. Catfish, can you help me unload it out of the back of my truck?"

A baby.

Here at Tanglewood.

Well, if that didn't beat all.

Since Ruby Prairie did not have a physician or a hospital, social worker Kim Beeson and policeman Mark Lister sat on hard, vinyl-covered chairs with Charlotte and Jock in the office waiting room of Dr. Sarah Strickland in Ella Louise, twenty miles from Ruby Prairie. Dr. Strickland had graciously agreed to come into her office at this odd time of night—if she hadn't, Charlotte knew, the four of them would be sitting in a Dallas hospital emergency room, cutting through endless red tape.

While they waited, Kim made cell phone calls to her supervisor.

Mark worked on his report.

Jock cracked his knuckles.

And Charlotte's mind raced.

A baby. At Tanglewood. At least until the child's mother could be found. What would the girls say? How did one take care of a newborn? He was probably hungry, though he hadn't cried at all on the drive over. Did that mean something was wrong? What if he was sick? Maybe the baby would have to go to the hospital after all. But who would stay with him? She couldn't leave the girls. Unless Treasure could stay with them.

Jock, who had been thumbing through a three-year-old copy of *Woman's Day*, stood up to pace and jingle the change in his pocket. After three times around the fifteen-by-fifteen-foot room, he planted himself at the front window, his expression fixed upon some distant spot outside in the dark.

From her seat, Charlotte studied his back. In the

window's reflection, she could see his closed eyes and moving lips. How tenderly he had cared for the little baby he'd found. He had held him in his arms in the car on the way over, fretting that no car seat was available, reminding her to drive carefully. Not until they had arrived at the clinic had he relinquished the bundle, and then only to Dr. Strickland.

Yes, Lord, Charlotte prayed too. *Be with us. Be with this child. Let him be all right. Be with his mother. Lord, what was she thinking leaving her baby on a cold, hard floor?*

Kim closed her phone. "We're all set for an emergency placement," she said. "Assuming everything checks out, the baby will go home with you tonight. I really appreciate this, Charlotte. I know you never planned to take children younger than nine. Will you be okay?"

"I think so," said Charlotte.

Jock turned.

"We'll be fine," said Charlotte, feigning confidence.

"Have you called Treasure?" asked Jock.

"I tried. Three times. Can't get the call to go through."

"Not surprised," said Mark. "Signal's terrible in Ruby Prairie."

"I know she's worried," said Charlotte. "All she knows is I had to go help Jock with something down at the church." She shot Jock a grin. "She probably figures we're setting up tables or something."

Jock came over and sat down again. "If you need

help—getting the girls to school in the morning or whatever—I'll be happy to pitch in."

"Thanks.

"'Course, what I really want to do is hold that baby while *you* take the girls to school."

"That might be arranged," said Charlotte. "But my guess is you'll have to stand in line to get a turn. Soon as word gets out that there's a baby at Tanglewood, half of Ruby Prairie will be on my doorstep, giving me advice and trying to get their hands on him."

Finally Dr. Strickland came out, carrying the baby in her arms.

"How is he?" asked Charlotte.

"Is he healthy?" asked Jock.

"How old is he?" asked Kim.

"The baby is fine," said Dr. Strickland. "Less than twenty-four hours old. Eight pounds, three ounces."

"But he's all right," said Jock.

"Except for one thing," said the doctor.

Charlotte drew a breath. "Something's wrong?"

"Not wrong, exactly."

Charlotte steeled herself for the worst.

"He's a she," said Dr. Strickland.

"What?" Charlotte looked at Jock.

"You mean—?" Jock looked at Charlotte.

Goodness. Neither of them had thought to look.

Chapter Five

After receiving instructions from Dr. Strickland about the care and feeding of the baby girl, Jock drove Charlotte to Tanglewood, where Treasure, Jasper, Kirby, and the girls, along with what appeared to be nearly half the helpful population of Ruby Prairie, waited.

The girls' reactions were mixed when Charlotte showed them the bundle in her arms.

"A baby!" Nikki said.

"Where'd you get her?" Sharita asked.

"Why's her face all scrunched up?" Vikki asked.

"She better not be dirty, 'cause I ain't changing no diapers," Maggie said.

"She's beautiful." Donna, mesmerized, gently touched the infant's tiny hand.

Jock, loath to leave the light, warmth, and disorganized bustle of Tanglewood, stayed until the baby was bathed, fed, burped, changed, and finally put to bed in the portable crib set up next to Charlotte's bed.

Charlotte let him help, which seemed only right. He was the one who had held the baby, talking to her and looking into her eyes for nearly an hour before Charlotte got to the church. Naturally he felt connected and responsible.

After the baby had fallen asleep, the girls had settled into their upstairs bedrooms, and everyone else had gone home, Jock lingered. Was there anything else Charlotte needed? Anything else he could do?

She assured him there was not. He had done enough. She was grateful. Did he want to drive her car home, since his truck was still at the church?

No. He would walk. He'd get the truck in the morning. It was no problem. The rain had stopped. He could use the fresh air.

Finally, after several false starts and more than twenty minutes in the entryway with his hand on the doorknob, he made it out to the porch. While Charlotte shivered and yawned, he continued to stall to the point of embarrassment before finally hiking home.

To his dark, too-quiet, too-empty house.

Once inside, still in his coat and gloves, he took a seat in his leather wingback—the one by his front window. Not even turning on a lamp, he sat staring out at the still, moonlit street in front of his house. Every house was dark. No wind blew. Not one car passed.

Jock rubbed his temples. He had a headache.

And his heart hurt.

For the baby?

Yes.

But for himself too. In the stillness of his house, Jock fought the growing ache of loneliness that had been plaguing him of late. He chided himself for being discontented.

Didn't he have a good life?

Of course he did.

Jock found joy in being a pastor and loved serving Lighted Way. Members of the church had, over the past six years, become like family. They lavished him with love and were good-naturedly tolerant of, if quick to point out, his missteps. Ruby Prairie's small-town idiosyncrasies kept him energized and entertained. His health was good. Thanks to a recent raise in salary, his finances were in fairly good shape. He even had a little put back.

God was good.

So why, after years of peace and contentment, was he feeling so restless, so like something was just not right, when everything in his life *was* right?

In the darkness of his living room, Jock knew.

It was Charlotte. Tanglewood. All those girls.

More and more often he found himself driving past the big pink Victorian, searching for and usually finding some lame excuse to stop in. On Sunday mornings and Wednesday evenings at Lighted Way, he caught himself watching for the arrival of Charlotte and her girls, responding with an increased heart rate and instantly wet palms when they finally bustled in. Around town, he could spot Charlotte's red van from two blocks away. How many times had he "accidentally on purpose" run into her? Just last week he counted three times at Rick's Grocery, twice at the 'Round the Clock Café, and once browsing at Sassy Clyde's antique store, Grandma Had One.

Which he had never done before in his life.

Jock chastised himself. He was acting like some lovesick fifteen-year-old. Hadn't the apostle Paul himself said that a man could better serve God alone? And hadn't Jock long ago come to the conclusion that he, like Paul, was the recipient of the gift of singleness?

Jock prayed well into the night.

The horses were fed and watered, and Kirby had boarded the bus to school. Jasper and Treasure had barely sat themselves down to share cups of quiet, midmorning coffee and cinnamon-dusted snickerdoodles when Jasper's volunteer ambulance pager went off. Its shrill buzz made Treasure jump.

"You're on call?" she asked. "I thought this was your three-day stretch off." But she got up, found his travel mug, filled it with a generous portion of the hot brew, then laced it with sugar and cream.

"It is. Jock's supposed to be on." Jasper was already struggling into his cowboy boots. "With all that's going on at Tanglewood, plus the Thanksgiving service, I told him to let me have it for the next few days."

"You have any students coming today?" she asked.

"None till after three." The pager went off again. "You heading to Tanglewood?"

"Soon as I can get dressed," said Treasure.

"Tell Charlotte I'm thinking about her. She and that baby are in my prayers." He pulled on his navy Ruby Prairie EMS jacket.

48

"Be careful. Call me." Treasure kissed her husband on the lips, handed him the mug, and tucked three warm, wrapped cookies into his jacket pocket.

"Thanks. Love you."

And he was out the door.

Treasure snagged the *Penny Saver* from the day's stacked mail, then leaned back in her recliner. She opened the weekly shopping rag to the business services section. Easy Perkins, the local sales representative, had talked her into purchasing a flashy, quarter-page ad.

"Shoot. Soon as this runs, you'll have more business than you'll know what to do with," Easy had assured her. "Mark my words, Miz Jones. Now that I think about it, you may as well go with my four-weeks-for-the-price-of-three rate. Save you a bundle."

This was the ad's second week to run. Her phone had yet to begin ringing off the hook. Treasure tried to imagine herself opening up the paper, reading the ad for the first time.

Stressed? In pain? Want to pamper yourself?
Try Treasure's Therapeutic Massage
Located in Lila's Beauty Shop, 1201 Main
Call for appointment

Nothing wrong, far as she could tell. Treasure tried not to fret, but back in Edmond, Oklahoma, where she'd moved from, she had been forced many times to turn away clients from her massage therapy clinic.

49

She'd been so busy her doctor had told her if she didn't cut back she would ruin her hands. Carpal tunnel syndrome. She flexed her hands and wrists. Thankfully that situation was much better.

Mayor Kerilynn Bell, always one to cheer on new Ruby Prairie businesses, had tried to encourage her.

"Sugar, you got to be patient. No one I know of has ever had a massage. Folks around here aren't sure about things they don't know much about."

At Kerilynn's invitation, Treasure had spoken at last month's Chamber of Commerce meeting, held at the 'Round the Clock.

Catfish Martin, Kerilynn's twin and owner of Ruby Prairie's only combination bait, snack, and video store, arrived just before the meeting started. Upon hearing his sister announce the program topic, he had come right out and said what other chamber members were thinking. "Massage therapy? Ain't that sort of thing illegal?"

"Catfish!" Kerilynn had shushed him. "It's our Treasure who's doing today's program."

"Jasper's wife? Well, I'll be."

Her program had gone well, Treasure thought. Carefully, she had explained the benefits of therapeutic massage, dispelled its myths, and even demonstrated by giving a chair massage to Kerilynn.

Yet despite her best educational efforts, Treasure had seen only a handful of paying clients since opening six weeks ago. She'd slashed her rates, changed her hours, offered three massages for the price of two. Her appointment book remained mostly blank.

Maybe she should look into direct mail.

Jock got a late start on what was sure to be a jam-packed day. It had been after two before he'd fallen asleep. He rolled out of bed and stretched his creaky back, then looked at his watch. Almost eight.

He should call Charlotte. See how things had gone last night. Perhaps she would need him to pick something up at the store. Cereal maybe. Didn't babies eat cereal? Rice? Maybe not this young.

No.

He would not call. Charlotte had plenty of help. Probably too much, if he knew Ruby Prairie. And baby or no baby, he had tons to get done in preparation for tonight's service. He still needed to work on his sermon. Check in with the committee chairs.

Kerilynn was in charge of food. Catfish was helping Alice and Nomie with decorating and general setting up. Gabe Eden and Dr. Lee Ross, Ruby Prairie's veterinarian, were making sure the building was ready and the grounds were looking their best.

Tonight's service, during which denominational differences were put aside, was one the entire community looked forward to every year. Folks came with their families and often invited their unchurched friends. Jock's desire was that the evening bring honor and glory to the Father, the giver of all good gifts.

Lord, help me to focus on today's tasks, Jock prayed.

I offer this day up to You. Use me to Your glory.

He poured himself a bowl of shredded wheat and microwaved water for instant coffee. As was his habit, he munched his bachelor breakfast while leaning against the counter and gazing out at the day through the window over his kitchen sink. Every yard on the street boasted trees covered with brilliantly colored leaves. Lester Collins, Ruby Prairie's resident amateur arborist, laid credit to a hot, dry summer followed by a late, rainy fall. Jock didn't know much about all that, but he agreed with Lester. This had to be one of the prettiest autumns in years.

As Jock chewed, a pair of playful squirrels in the yard of Mrs. Lavada Castle, the widow across the street, caught his eye. They raced and chased each other around the trio of red-leafed sweetgums in the yard of the old woman, whom everyone in Ruby Prairie affectionately referred to as Miss Lavada. Jock's eyes followed one of the furry creatures up a tree, then caught sight of something that caused him to choke on a fiber-filled bite.

There was a ladder leaned up against the eaves of the home's flat-roofed carport. And slowly, unsteadily ascending that ladder was eighty-seven-year-old Miss Lavada herself.

What in the world was she thinking?

Not taking time to put on his shoes, Jock hotfooted it out his door and raced across the yard. He had not even made it across the street when he saw Miss Lavada pause, sway like a reed in the wind, and go down.

• • •

Nomie Jenkins, Alice Buck, and Ginger Collins arrived at Tanglewood before six to cook breakfast, make sandwiches for sack lunches, and help Charlotte get the girls off to school. Though helpful, their efforts were not enough.

Eight fifteen.

Nikki couldn't find her left shoe.

Maggie's ponytail kept coming out lumpy.

Vikki had spent ten minutes trying to convince Charlotte that a sundress *was* appropriate November wear.

Sharita stopped up the upstairs toilet.

And Donna feigned a sore throat in a dramatic effort to stay home.

All while Charlotte was trying to feed, burp, and diaper the baby while keeping her lap dry.

After several false starts, a few tears, and two near-total meltdowns, Nomie and Alice were finally able to herd the girls into Tanglewood's van, where Ginger's husband, Lester, waited to drive them to school.

Nomie and Alice left, and Ginger stayed behind to tidy up the kitchen until Lester got back.

Charlotte, still in her pink flannel pajamas and lime green slipper socks, held the baby in her arms. She parted the living room's lace curtains and watched as the van rolled out of sight. *Be with them, Lord. Don't give them anything they can't handle today. Hold them in Your hands.*

Her girls didn't take well to change. Though they all

appeared fascinated by the new arrival, she still represented a threat to every one of them. Her newborn's cuteness and urgent needs only made the situation more difficult. Charlotte knew what to expect.

Nikki and Vikki would whine and cling.

Maggie, remarkably apt in her ability to hurt everyone's feelings in an amazingly short span of time, would get loud and say hateful things, then feign innocence at the tears she prompted.

Donna would withdraw and complain that she couldn't sleep.

Sharita would step up her assertions that Charlotte did not treat her the same as the other girls because she was black.

And every one of the girls would act out in school. They would talk back to their teachers, pick fights with their classmates, try to cheat on tests, and lose their homework. So frequently did Ben Jackson, principal of the public school, have something to report, that Charlotte suspected him of having Tanglewood's number on speed dial.

Foster parent training had prepared her for the behaviors of a houseful of troubled girls. Extensive reading had given her insight into the growth and development of adolescents. Attending workshops helped equip her for the running of her home.

But nothing, nothing had prepared her for how much she would love them. By the time each of the girls had gotten out of Kim Beeson's car and made it halfway up the sidewalk leading to Tanglewood's front steps,

Charlotte had been head-over-heels committed.

Won't it break your heart when she leaves? she had been asked by at least a half-dozen friends, back when Beth was preparing to leave for prep school in Colorado.

Yes, Charlotte had said with conviction. *It will break my heart. And that will mean that I did my job right.*

She let the curtain fall and stood looking down into the wide, unblinking eyes of the baby in her arms. She was so tiny. So perfect. And so fragile.

Ginger called from the kitchen. "Sugar, I've put a roast in the Crock-Pot and started some bread mix in your machine. There's a load of clothes in the washer and one in the dryer. Lester's stopping at Rick's after he drops the girls off. You're about out of milk and completely out of paper towels. Is there anything else you can think of that you need? I can call Rick and leave a message."

Charlotte moved from the window to stand in front of the living room fire, rocking the baby back and forth with an instinctual swaying of her body. "Not a thing. I appreciate you so much. This morning would have been impossible without you and Nomie and Alice and Lester."

Ginger dried her hands on a tea towel, then came close to stroke the baby's little head. "I can't imagine a mother who could leave a sweet little thing like this. Precious. She is just too precious," Ginger cooed. "And she is blessed to have you."

For a long moment neither woman spoke. Neither of

55

them could tear her eyes from the baby's face. Finally Charlotte broke the silence.

"J.D. and I were never able to have children. We tried for years. I've often wondered how different our lives would have been if we'd been able to have a baby."

"You're a good mother to these girls," said Ginger softly. "You make it look easy."

"It's not easy," said Charlotte. "I make lots of mistakes."

"You would have been a wonderful mother to a child of your own."

"I don't know," said Charlotte. A single tear rolled down her face. "I guess it would have been nice to have had a chance to try."

Chapter Six

How bad's she hurt?" Gabe Eden was the first one out of the ambulance and to the elderly woman's side. Jasper, toting the heavy EMS supply bag and the bright orange backboard, trotted close behind.

"She's not conscious, but she's breathing and she's got a pulse," said Jock. In his sock feet, shivering in plaid flannel pajama pants and a gray T-shirt, he knelt in the wet leaves beside Miss Lavada. He had not moved from the woman's side since calling 9-1-1. To the sound of every dog in the neighborhood barking, and with the wafting smell of someone's breakfast bacon, Jock had stroked Miss Lavada's hand and talked softly in her ear, all the while praying for her to be okay.

Though it took Gabe and Jasper less than fifteen minutes to get from home to the station to the Castle residence, by the time he spotted the ambulance Jock felt as if he'd been waiting half a day. He kept thinking someone would drive by, see the two of them on the ground beside her carport, and stop, but no one did. Where were Catfish and his scanner when you needed them?

"You see her fall?" asked Gabe.

"Yes," said Jock. "I looked out my kitchen window and saw her climbing that ladder. I ran out to stop her, but before I could get to her, she was already down."

"This how she landed?" asked Jasper. He applied a cervical collar, covered her with a blanket, then began to take Miss Lavada's vital signs.

"I haven't moved her."

"What in the world was she thinking? Eighty-something years old and up on a ladder." Jasper shook his head.

"Last I heard, her kids been thinking she might be getting a touch of the old-timer's disease," said Gabe. "Bless her heart." He lifted Miss Lavada's lids to shine a bright light in each of her eyes. "Equal. Reactive." He ran his hands over her scalp. "Got a big knot right on the back of her head. Can't find that it's

57

broken the skin. No blood. You fellows see any other injuries?"

"This right arm may be broken," said Jasper. He applied a splint.

"Best to load and go," said Gabe.

Jock moved the backboard into position beside the woman.

"Pastor," said Gabe, "you reckon you could call some of her family?"

"Of course."

"Can't imagine Miz Lavada's got her house locked, but if it is, I happen to know there's a key in a peanut can hid behind that bush to the right of her front door," said Gabe. "You should be able to find some numbers somewhere inside."

"No problem. I'll check her stove and all to make sure nothing's been left on; then I'll lock it up tight," said Jock.

"Gentlemen," said Jasper, "let's get going."

The three of them positioned themselves to slide Miss Lavada onto the backboard. "On three," said Gabe. "One. Two—"

"Lord Jesus." Miss Lavada groaned and opened her eyes. "What in heaven's name are you doing to me?"

"Miz Lavada, it's me. Gabe Eden. With the ambulance service. You've taken a fall. We're carrying you to the hospital."

She tried to sit up. "Young man, I don't know where your ball is. Now take this thing off my neck. I have to go home."

"No, ma'am," said Jasper, louder than Gabe. "We have to leave that on. We're putting you in the ambulance. Your arm looks to be broken."

"I don't know anything about any farm," said Miss Lavada. "I was raised all my life in town. Now you let me up right this minute, or I'll call the police."

Gabe and Jasper cast glances at Jock. He moved from his position at her feet up to her head.

"Pastor?" Miss Lavada's watery gray eyes registered recognition. She reached up to smooth her flyaway white hair. "What are you doing here? Aren't you supposed to be at the church?"

"Yes, ma'am. I'm going there in just a minute. Getting ready for the Thanksgiving service tonight."

"That's real nice," said Miss Lavada—like there was not one thing unusual about lying in a pile of wet leaves having a conversation with the preacher. "I'm making three pies. One coconut, one chocolate, and one pecan. You know my trees have been just loaded with pecans this year. Picked up all the ones on the ground, but got to collect those off the roof of my garage before the squirrels get to them." She tried again to get up.

"That's just wonderful. You make the best pies I've ever eaten in my life."

"Oh, Pastor." She reached up and patted his cheek. "You're kind to say that. Secret's in the crust. I use pure lard."

"Really? I would have never guessed." Jock placed his hand on her uninjured arm. "Now about those

59

pecans. How about I gather them? You go with Gabe and Jasper and let the doctor look at your arm. I'll have those pecans in your kitchen when you get back home."

Miss Lavada's spell of clear thinking passed. She shrugged Jock's arm away and began to thrash. "What do you think I am? A banker. I can't give you a loan. Who are you? Let me up. I'm an old woman. It's not right for you to treat me this way. Help! Help!"

Gabe looked at his watch.

Jasper shifted from one wet knee to the other.

Lord, forgive me, prayed Jock. "Sister Lavada," he said in his most authoritative, stained-glass voice. "Stop it. Listen to me. I have a word from the Lord. Jesus says for you to go to the hospital. He says for you to go in the ambulance. Right now. Do you understand?"

For an instant Miss Lavada stopped her squirming and looked into his eyes. "Pastor, you tell Jesus that I can't go anywhere like this." She lowered her voice. "I'm not properly attired. You tell the Lord that He should know me better than that. Pastor, I'm not wearing a slip."

Jock sat on a back pew of the empty, unlit sanctuary, enjoying a quick moment of quiet. In just over an hour the pews in front of him would be filled with believers from various Ruby Prairie churches—all come together to offer their autumn thanks to God.

What a day it had been. Lots of distractions, several

60

mishaps. Miss Lavada. A paper plate shortage. Some kind of a crisis with the pumpkin pies. His phone had rung at least twenty times.

Jock leaned back and breathed in deeply, appreciating the clean scent of the two dozen pots of yellow, gold, and bronze mums that adorned the pulpit area. Amazing. Lighted Way's plain-looking interior had been transformed. Along with the mums, pumpkins and gourds of various sizes added bright color to the usually unadorned space at the front. Pew ends were decorated with Indian corn affixed to small grapevine wreaths tied with multicolored raffia ribbons.

The outside of the church looked festive too. He'd come in the front door just to see how it would look to arriving visitors. A larger grapevine wreath, decorated in much the same manner as the ones on the pews, adorned the sanctuary door. Two dozen tall candle sconces, ready to be lit, lined the sidewalk. Jock had been duly impressed when Catfish told him he'd made the sconces out of empty tuna cans, scrap pipe, and black spray paint.

"Didn't cost nothing but for the paint," Catfish had explained.

The slightest aroma of tuna lingered, which explained the four stray cats Jock spotted lurking near the front door.

The fellowship hall had bustled with activity all day. Kerilynn and her crew had done an incredible job orchestrating the mouth-watering spread. Since three o'clock, a steady stream of members had dropped off

61

their contributions of pies, salads, and side dishes. Since they were being cooked on site, the smell of roasting turkeys and baking corn-bread dressing tantalized Jock each time he stepped inside the hall. What a hardworking group of folks he served.

Sitting in the quiet, he wondered about Charlotte. About the baby. He'd thought of them off and on all day but hadn't had a moment to call. He doubted she'd be here tonight, since the baby was so young. Someone else would pick up the Tanglewood girls. Most likely Ginger and Lester. Then again, their grandkids were in—all six of them. They would have their hands full. Probably Treasure and Jasper would drive the girls over.

Jock leaned his head forward to rest on the pew in front of him. *Lord, be with us this evening. Help our hearts to be focused upon You and all the blessings You've given us. Thank You for all the hands that worked so unselfishly to make this evening special. Bless everyone who comes tonight. Be with the choir, the ushers, the ladies who'll serve the food. Be with me. May the words I speak tonight be words of hope, of peace, of truth. In Jesus' name, I pray. Amen.*

They were going to be late. So late that Charlotte wondered if she and the girls should go to the Thanksgiving service at all. If not for the fact that Sharita was singing a solo—thankfully, she was already at the church—Charlotte might have decided they should all stay home. How was it that one additional member of the household, one who weighed less than nine pounds, could precipitate such chaos?

She'd started the day with an organized plan, albeit after only five hours of sleep. It wasn't as though she hadn't had help. Lester, even though he and Ginger had a houseful of grandkids for the weekend, picked the girls up from school. Treasure spent much of the day at Tanglewood showing Charlotte how to most efficiently take care of the baby.

There was so much to learn.

Who knew a newborn didn't *always* burp?

Or that more than one dirty diaper in a day was normal?

Or that bottles of formula didn't *have* to be warmed up?

If not for everyone's help, Charlotte figured she would still be in her pajamas. As it was, she'd barely gotten herself dressed, combed her hair, and brushed her teeth.

Time was when she would have asserted her independence and attempted to take care of the new addition all on her own. Not anymore. Though she was still self-reliant by nature, nearly losing Tanglewood last year had all but cured Charlotte of the belief that she and the Lord could go it alone. When she was at her lowest, overwhelmed by one crisis after another, Ruby Prairie citizens were the helping hands of God, ministering to her and her girls.

Softening her independent stance had been tough for

someone like Charlotte—someone who, after losing both parents in a car crash during her freshman year in college, had learned to depend upon no one but herself. Even during her twenty-year marriage, she had been loath to rely upon anyone but herself. Which, looking back, was not a completely bad thing, since when J.D. got sick with cancer, Charlotte had needed to take care of everything.

Wasn't it amazing how, even in her heartbreak, God had worked things out?

Jock had said God teaches us what we need to know to get through the next thing. And once that lesson is learned, it's most likely time to go on to something else. He believed that God wasn't One to leave His people the same.

Lord, what would You have me to learn now? Charlotte prayed. *I'm confused and nervous, and I don't know what I'm doing.*

One last diaper change. One more little burp. She zipped up the baby into a pink terry sleeper and placed her in the seat she would strap into the van. The girls were waiting, already outside and buckled in. Charlotte fumbled with the seat's straps. In her coat, she began to sweat. She tried to fasten the latch, but couldn't make the thing snap into place. Her back hurt from bending over. How did this thing hook? It had seemed so easy when she'd watched Jock do it. She should have paid better attention.

Wide-eyed and unblinking, the baby tolerated Charlotte's awkward maneuvering, her shifting of the seat, her repeated frustrated tries. The latch wouldn't budge.

Charlotte fought the urge to cry.

It was too much.

All of it.

Over the years Charlotte had played with other people's children. She'd tended babies when her turn came around to keep the church nursery. She even babysat on occasion for the children of friends who needed to go out. Despite her best efforts, over and over she'd felt the indulgent but hurtful bemusement of *real* mothers when they observed her awkwardness—her inexperienced attempts to apply a diaper that wouldn't leak, to produce a burp without getting spit up on, to snap up a sleeper so that the legs came out even. She'd endured good-natured jokes about her ineptitude, laughing along, making fun of herself, while hiding from them her acute embarrassment, her envy of their ease.

How did one obtain that gentle smoothness, that choreographed, do-three-things-at-once motherly dance? How did one learn to know what a baby needed before he even began to fret? Was it something inborn?

Something she didn't have?

Charlotte stood up to straighten her complaining back. She looked down into the baby's wide eyes and prayed, *Do You intend for me to care for this baby, Lord? For how long?*

There'd been no call from Kim all day.

I'm not very good at this. It's harder than it looks. And Lord, what if I fall in love with her? It's so hard taking care of her, but what about when she has to leave? Will You give me the strength?

Honk. Honk.

The baby jumped.

Those girls. The van's horn halted Charlotte's meandering prayers. As if on cue, the right strap snapped into the right latch, and the baby was secure. What had she done differently? She had no clue.

Thank You, Lord, for this one thing.

With the baby's seat in one hand, she slung her purse onto her other shoulder. Yes. Her hand found the van key, right in the little pocket where it belonged.

"Okay," she said to the baby. "Little one, they're waiting for us. You ready for your first visit to church?"

The baby appeared to be sleeping.

Charlotte looked at the clock. They might not be so late after all.

But then the smell of a diaper in dire need of a change reached Charlotte's unpowdered nose.

Late after all.

Chapter Seven

Jock, dressed in chocolate brown slacks and a cream-colored sweater, stood in the pulpit and looked out over the crowd of worshipers.

The Baptists had made a good showing.

So had the Methodists.

As had the Pentecostals.

In the sea of faces, a few caught Jock's eyes. On the third pew from the front, Lester and Ginger Collins settled in, sandwiching their six squirmy grandchildren between them.

Near the far left wall sat Joe Fazoli. Joe was Catholic. Since Ruby Prairie had no Catholic church, Joe was a frequent, if sometimes confused, visitor at Lighted Way. Jock saw that Joe's out-of-town cousin was with him. Good. The fellow was an awesome guitar player. His presence meant music would be on the menu at Joe's restaurant for the next few nights.

Behind Joe and his cousin sat Treasure, Jasper, and Kirby.

Over on the right was Sassy Clyde, next to Alice Buck.

In uniform and sitting in the back pew, in case he got a call, Officer Mark Lister shifted a bit in his seat.

Near the front, on the left, were half a dozen residents of New Energy, accompanied by two scrub-suited nurse's aides. Jock had seen the nursing home's van out back. How good that they had been able to come—even if three of the six had already nodded off.

Lighted Way's sanctuary was so full that Catfish and Gabe were moving chairs in from the Sunday school classrooms and placing them in the aisles for late-comers. Jock could hear their exaggerated whispers as they tried to place the chairs with minimal disruption.

Kerilynn and her kitchen crew, he knew, were back in the fellowship hall hurriedly cutting pieces of pie in half to make sure there would be enough dessert to go around. Lee Ross had left to go get more ice.

The abundant turnout was a blessing, but Jock hoped his members' acts of service didn't cause them to miss out on what they'd worked so hard to prepare.

Because it was past time to begin.

"Welcome," Jock said. "On behalf of the members of Lighted Way Church, I offer thanks to all of you for coming. May the Lord be pleased with our worship this evening. May each of us here be uplifted by our coming together. We have many things to be thankful for. As some of you know, our Mrs. Lavada Castle fell this morning. It could have been bad, but I'm happy to report that though she's shook up and very sore, she has no broken bones."

The door at the back opened, then closed, then opened again. Finally, in filed Nikki and Vikki, Donna, Maggie, Sharita, and Charlotte with the baby in her arms. Before she could get them all settled down, the infant began to cry, causing half of the worshipers to turn around to look.

"Tanglewood has been blessed too," said Jock. "Yesterday, a newborn baby was found abandoned here at the church."

Folks who hadn't heard gasped, then turned to their neighbors to ask for whispered details.

"It's a little girl," said Jock. "As you can hear, one with a good, strong set of lungs."

Charlotte blushed and fumbled in the diaper bag for a pacifier.

"She's in Charlotte Carter's care at Tanglewood. While we grieve for this situation and pray for her parents, we are so thankful the baby was found safe and healthy."

"Amen," said the Baptists.

"Yes, Lord," said the Pentecostals.

"Wahhh," said the baby.

The Methodists nodded their heads.

Kerilynn, Dr. Ross, Catfish, and Gabe—missions accomplished—took folding chairs near the back.

Pastor Jock motioned for the youth choir to come forward. Dressed in red-satin-trimmed black robes and sneakers, they moved to their places. As one, they shuffled first to the right and then to the left. They fumbled with their music and dropped at least two sets before finally, on cue, opening their mouths to sing.

As the sounds of the sweet young worshipers fell upon their ears, the congregation moved into a mood of awe and reverence. First, "To God Be the Glory," followed by "Count Your Blessings." Jock could feel a peace and stillness settle over the group.

The congregation stood to sing "We Gather Together."

Then Sharita, dreadlocks pulled back from her lovely face, the color of coffee laced with cream, stepped forward to sing "Praise God from Whom All Blessings Flow." She pulled none of her usual shenanigans—made no faces, did no little dance, did not toss her head or swish her hips. Instead, she threw her head back, closed her eyes, and made her body still. After only the slightest pause, notes rich and full as molten gold began to slowly flow from her mouth.

While Sharita sang, no one moved. Jock wasn't sure anyone even breathed. How a person so young and raw as Sharita could sing like such an angel could only be explained by the presence of God. Few dry eyes remained in the pews by the time she sat down.

To Jock's mind, every one of the worshipers could have left right then, having gotten what they'd come for. Reluctantly he took his place in the pulpit to speak.

His sermon was a short one, full of illustrations, stories, and Scripture. While many in the pews were regular churchgoers, there were also lots of visitors in attendance, as well as many children. Tonight marked the beginning of the time of year when people's hearts were more tuned to spiritual things.

"Like the child in Charlotte's arms," he began, "we too were once abandoned and lost. And while we are thankful for many, many things—our health, our friends, our families—it is the fact that we have been found that prompts us to lift our voices in praise to our Father."

"Yes, Lord," said the Pentecostals.

"Amen," agreed the Baptists.

From what Jock could see, hear, and sense (if he didn't count the nodding New Energy folks), his words were falling upon mostly attentive ears. After eighteen years as a pastor, he had developed acute awareness of every movement, whisper, and clandestinely opened peppermint. At this moment, he registered three people with coughs, some shuffling middle schoolers in the back section, and a woman on the left digging in her purse. Not bad.

"God loves us. The greatest gift He ever gave us was His Son. Rather than caring about us from afar, He came to love us where we are, as we are. For that we are most thankful."

Jock found himself only slightly distracted by a frantic whispered commotion going on in the third row. Two wriggly Collins grandsons apparently needed to go.

Now. Their faces bore the strained, impossible-to-ignore looks that recently potty-trained three-year-olds adopt at the most inopportune moments. When Lester reluctantly got up to take the boys out, he caught Jock's eye and shot him an apologetic look.

Jock didn't miss a beat. What was a church without children? He would take the antics of toddlers, the

71

cries of babies, and the disruption of note-writing teenagers any day over a sanctuary full of well-behaved old people.

Lester and the boys were gone a pretty long while. Long enough that Ginger began turning around to see if he was coming back. "Where's Grandpa?" Jock heard one of the granddaughters ask.

His sermon neared its end.

Finally the three reappeared and started their way back down to their seats. The boys tumbled down the center aisle like plump puppies. When they reached their pew, they plopped down right on the end, their little legs straight out, feet against the pew in front of them. Lester, standing in the aisle, whispered to the tots to scoot.

Neither boy budged.

Jock could feel the congregation's focus shift from his message to Lester and the adorable, amusing little boys. He paused.

"Move over, son," whispered Lester, his face slightly pink. "Grandpa can't get in. Move over closer to your sister."

But the boys had exciting news. News that could not wait.

"Grandma!" one squealed. "Guess what!"

"Shhh," whispered Ginger. She motioned for the boys to move down.

"Grandpa potty too! Grandpa potty too!" the other boy shouted.

As the entire congregation moved from muffled

72

snorts to uncontrolled guffaws, Jock grinned and nodded to poor Lester, who had managed to push his grandsons in enough that he could sit down.

Jock closed his Bible and ended the sermon with a smile and a shrug. "What can I say, folks? The message is yours. Thank God for kids."

"Amen," chuckled the Baptists.

"Yes, Lord," hee-hawed the Pentecostals.

"Uh-huh," agreed the Methodists, wiping tears from their eyes.

"Shall we stand and sing?" suggested Jock. "Then Gabe Eden, deacon here at Lighted Way, will lead us in a final prayer of thanksgiving, including thanks for the meal we're about to eat."

The delicious smells of roast turkey, corn-bread dressing, and homemade yeast-risen rolls enticed even those worshipers who'd not intended to stay for the meal. In Lighted Way's well-lit, overheated fellowship hall, the sound level rose to such a decibel that folks found themselves nearly shouting to be heard by the person standing right next to them. Children, taking advantage of their parents' diverted attention, squealed and chased each other between sets of adult knees.

Kerilynn and her crew, armed with hefty serving spoons, scurried into position. When they were ready, she gave Jock the signal. "This way," she directed without leaving her post. She didn't have to call twice.

Despite Charlotte's instructions to her girls, Nikki

and Vikki, Donna, Sharita, and Maggie were among those first to go through the line.

"Hello, girls," said Kerilynn. "Paper plates are down here. Desserts and tea at the other end. Y'all start this way and move down the line."

Charlotte, from the last amen, was swarmed by Ruby Prairie folks wanting to see the baby and hear all the details.

"You mean they still don't know who her parents are?"

"How old is she?"

"How long will you have her?"

"What will happen if they don't find her mama?"

"Bless her little heart."

"How are the other girls taking to a little one in the house?"

"You need help, sugar, you call and let me know."

"You ever seen such a pretty baby, Pastor?"

Charlotte, busy wiping spit-up from the baby's chin, looked up. Jock had snaked his way through the throng to join the admiring crowd.

"She's beautiful," he agreed. "Just beautiful." He motioned to the other end of the hall. "You ladies better have some of Kerilynn's famous turkey and dressing," he said. "Looks like the line's moving pretty well."

"You're right, Pastor. We don't want to miss out."

"Hope there's still some of Ginger Collins's pie left. She makes the best pecan I've ever eaten. Someone told me she puts a touch of cinnamon in her crust."

"Cinnamon? I never heard of such."

"Charlotte, you want us to fix you a plate?"

"That would be great. Thank you."

"Honey, you want sweet or unsweet?"

"Unsweet, please."

The ladies dispersed. Charlotte, relieved to no longer be the center of attention, shifted the baby from one tired arm to the other. She scanned the crowd. Where were the girls? Were they behaving themselves?

Jock caught her eye. "They're fine. See? At that table over on the right. Next to Catfish. He'll keep them in line." He motioned for Charlotte to sit down in a folding chair, then pulled one up for himself. "Can I hold her?"

"She's been spitting up a lot. I may have to change her formula."

"That's okay."

Charlotte handed the baby over, then was amazed at how light her arms felt when she straightened out her elbows and flexed her wrists. She looked down. Goodness. Her blouse was buttoned crooked. She tried to discreetly fix it, one mother-of-pearl button at a time.

"How's it going?" asked Jock. He placed the blanket-wrapped baby in the crook of his crossed knee. "I wanted to call you all day, but I didn't get the chance."

"You've had a bit on your own plate today," said Charlotte. "The service was wonderful. Everything looks nice. And your message, at least the part I heard, was great."

"It's a good turnout. And Kerilynn outdid herself with the meal." He stroked the baby's chin. "Any word?"

"Not one. I expected a call from Kim. Every time the phone rang I jumped."

"Why wouldn't she call?"

"Her caseload is heavy," said Charlotte. "You know how they say that with God a day is as a thousand years, and a thousand years is as a day? In that one way, caseworkers are sort of like God. I was supposed to have Nikki and Vikki for three months. Sharita's placement was initially to be for only a few weeks. It's the same with all the girls." She paused. "Not that I'm complaining."

"Still," said Jock, "you'd think calling you would be priority, since you only agreed to keep the baby on a temporary, emergency basis."

"The truth is that Kim probably doesn't have any news," said Charlotte. "And my best guess is that she doesn't have anyone else willing. There's a huge shortage of foster homes."

Jock's eyes locked on Charlotte's. "What if they can't find another placement for her?"

Charlotte's eyes filled. She was grateful that, for the moment, no one else was around. "What do you think?" She dug in the diaper bag for a tissue.

"I think it's time you started calling this little girl something other than 'the baby,' " said Jock, "because I believe you're going to have her for a while."

76

Chapter Eight

The aroma of a microwaved Lean Cuisine and the recorded sound of Elvis Presley greeted Treasure when she pushed open the door of Lila Peterson's storefront beauty shop. It was located on Main, next door to Hardy's Hardware; customers entered Lila's through a door the beautician had painted bright yellow, then adorned with a hand-stenciled green vine. The windows on each side of the yellow door were hung with white eyelet-trimmed café curtains. During summer months, planters underneath those windows brimmed with marigolds, English ivy, and red geraniums. Today they held lanky, in-need-of-water yellow and purple pansies. Taped eye level in the window to the left of the door was a hand-lettered sign:

Therapeutic Massage by Treasure Jones
Tuesday–Friday
Call for appointment. Walk-ins welcome.
Special introductory price: One-hour massage, $25.00

Both the shampoo chair and the styling station were empty. So was the rest of the tiny front room of the shop.

"Yoo hoo," Treasure called. She wiped her feet on the mat.

Lila, her mouth full, came through the floral curtain that separated her work area from the back. "You caught me," she said after swallowing. "Had lunch? Got an extra frozen dinner. Glazed chicken, I think."

"No, thanks." Treasure slipped out of her coat and hung it up on the rack.

"How about some cake?" said Lila. "Ginger Collins brought me half a cream cheese pound cake."

"We have any coffee?"

"Hazelnut. Picked up a bag at Rick's this morning. Smells heavenly. You want me to make us a pot?"

Treasure eyed the bag. "Fancy. I'm impressed. Sit down and finish your lunch; I'll put the coffee on. And yes, ma'am, I'll have some of Ginger's cake. 'Course, rich as it is, I may as well apply it directly to my thighs." She filled the coffee carafe with water from the shampoo sink. "When's your next appointment?"

"Three. Gabe Eden for a haircut. After him, Alice Buck's coming for a perm."

Treasure opened her pristine appointment book. She sighed.

"Maybe you'll have a walk-in," said Lila.

"Maybe. I brought my crocheting so as to have something to do, but if things don't pick up soon, I'm going to pull that sign down."

"Don't get discouraged," said Lila—the same thing she'd said every Tuesday, Wednesday, Thursday, and Friday of the past month. "Not yet anyway."

Treasure had completed a dozen rows on her afghan by the time Alice came in for her perm.

"Lands," said Alice. She pulled off her sweater and settled herself into the shampoo chair. "I've just come from New Energy. Went out there to help with bingo. Got a new little activity director. Sweet as can be, but child's so soft-spoken none of the residents can hear what numbers she's called. She's got ever' one of them thinking they need to get the batteries changed in their hearing aids."

"How's Miss Lavada?" asked Lila.

"Oh, honey, she's not doing well at all. Hates it there. Wants to go home."

"How long she have to stay?" asked Treasure.

"Since she didn't break any bones, likely only a few weeks. Problem is, she's having lots of pain. Still all stove up. Won't take her exercises. Says the therapist is trying to kill her."

"Bless her heart," said Lila.

"Until she's up and moving better, doctor says he won't let her go home," said Alice. "Poor thing's depressed is what I think. Taking who-knows-what-all kinds of pain medicine. I don't know what they're going to do with her."

"She still confused?" asked Treasure.

"Hard to tell," said Alice. "I heard her kids thought she might have a touch of Alzheimer's, but I don't think so. 'Course, she's forgetful and deaf as a post, so it's not exactly easy to know what's going on in that mind of hers. Miss Lavada's always been a bit of a character. You know she used to raise peacocks?"

"Really?" said Lila. She wrapped a leopard-print plastic cape around Alice.

"Bred 'em. Made pretty good money. Packed little peacock chicks up in boxes with airholes and mailed them all over the U.S."

"You mean she took live birds to the post office?" Treasure had never heard of such a thing. "That's legal?"

"I don't know about legal," said Alice. "All I'm saying is Miss Lavada used to do it. I asked her one time how it was those chicks survived. She told me she didn't know, but that over the years most every bird she shipped made it to where they were going without any trouble."

"She's a character, all right," said Lila. "Alice, I need you to lean back just a little bit more, honey."

Treasure worked a couple more rows. "You know," she said, after Lila had moved Alice from the shampoo station to the styling chair, "I believe I might could help Miss Lavada, maybe relieve some of her pain. Least make her feel better. You think she'd let me try?"

"I bet she would," said Alice, who so far had not let Treasure give her a massage. "Long as you approached her right. Take her a cheeseburger from the 'Round the Clock when you go. She loves Keri-lynn's burgers. Fries wouldn't hurt either."

"That would be so sweet of you to do that," said Lila.

80

"You think the nursing home would allow it?" asked Treasure. "Even though massage isn't considered a medical procedure, they'd need to check with her doctor."

"I can't imagine that they'd have a problem with it," said Alice. "Lila, hand me that phone. Rose Ann Eden's the director of nursing. I'll call her right now and ask."

"I think we should call her Rikki," said Vikki.

Charlotte and the girls had finished supper. Pizza from Joe's. The girls, herded from the table to the living room by Charlotte, sprawled in front of the fire.

"That's a boy's name," said Maggie. It was her turn to hold the baby. Nestled into one of the living room's sofas, she touched the infant's forehead. "You don't want a boy's name, do you, baby?"

"Watch her soft spot," said Donna. Sitting next to Maggie, she'd already had her turn.

"We should name her Britney," said Sharita. "Like for Britney Spears. She's so pretty. What you talking about—a soft spot? She's soft all over."

"There's a soft place on the top of her head. It's where the parts of her skull haven't formed yet," explained Charlotte. She added a log to the fire, poked at it until it began to flame, then eased down on the other side of Maggie. "Babies' heads are soft so that they can be flexible when they're born. It's a pretty tight squeeze for a baby when it comes out of its mother."

81

"That's gross," said Sharita.

"How does a baby get out of its mother?" asked Nikki.

"You know!" said Vikki. "Remember?" She whispered in her twin's ear.

"Oh, yeah," said Nikki. She turned pink. "Now I remember."

Sharita rolled her eyes.

Charlotte continued. "Even though we don't know how long she'll be here, I think it's time we gave her a name."

"How we know she don't already got a name?" asked Maggie. "Maybe her mama gave her a name and we just don't know it."

"She don't got no mama," said Sharita. "That's why she's here."

Donna pulled her feet up under her and wrapped her arms around her knees.

"Least you got a daddy," said Sharita. "The baby don't got neither."

"You're right," said Charlotte to Maggie. "She may already have a name. Problem is, we don't know what it is, so I thought we could give her one for now. Sort of like a nickname. Don't you think we should call her something besides 'the baby'?"

"She needs a name," agreed Maggie. "But not Britney. What about Chelsea? That's a pretty name."

"That's a dumb name," said Nikki.

"Not as dumb as Nikki," said Maggie.

"Girls. Stop it," said Charlotte.

"I think we should call her Molly," said Vikki.

"Molly," said Charlotte. "That's pretty. What do y'all think?"

"I like it," said Maggie. "Better than Britney, but not as good as Chelsea."

"I think Molly is a pretty name," said Donna.

"We should vote," said Sharita. "Raise your hand if you think we should name the baby Molly."

Half a dozen hands went up. Nikki and Vikki, each holding a cat, raised the animals' front paws.

"Okay then," said Charlotte. "I think we've picked out a good name."

Maggie, still holding the baby, raised her hand after the voting was done.

"What's the matter?" asked Charlotte. "I thought you liked the name Molly."

"I do," said Maggie, her nose wrinkled up. "What I wanna tell you is that I think Molly needs her diaper changed."

It was after ten before Charlotte got the girls off to their upstairs bedrooms. She reminded the twins to brush their teeth. She prompted Sharita and Maggie to pick out tomorrow's school clothes. Balancing Molly in her arms, she went into Donna's room.

Sharita's comments about the baby not having a mother had rubbed at Donna's wounds. She was tearful and clingy, stalling, wanting to talk. Bless her heart. They'd been through this many nights before. There were no good words to be said. How did one explain a mother abandoning her child?

Charlotte gently rubbed Donna's back, then bent to wipe a tear. "I know," she whispered. "Honey, I know." Then she sat stroking Donna's hair until the girl fell asleep.

Soon after the other girls were settled in, Charlotte fed Molly and put her to bed in the bassinet in her bedroom. After turning on the baby monitor, she made herself a cup of peppermint tea and returned to the living room to soak up a few moments of quiet. She let her mind roam while the flames in the fireplace turned the wood to embers and then to ash.

Ten days had passed since Jock had found Molly. A week and a half of nearly everyday just-thought-I-would-stop-by visits from him. Charlotte was amazed at how good Jock was with the newborn, relaxed and comfortable in ways one would not expect from a man who'd never had a child of his own. He was willing, even eager, to feed her, burp her, even to change the most aromatic of diapers.

He'd been at Tanglewood the day Kim brought over papers for Charlotte to fill out, enabling her to care for the baby legally. Until the arrival of Molly, Charlotte had intended, and been licensed, to care for children ages nine to eighteen. Kim admitted she did not know how long Molly would be at Tanglewood. A few weeks? Months? Lots depended upon whether her parents were found. The system moved slowly. While she and Kim discussed what lay ahead, Jock held Molly in his arms.

Charlotte wanted—needed—to know how long she would have Molly in her care. She'd not felt that deep, almost panicky desire for a timetable with any of the other girls. The essence of fostering was its temporary nature. She knew that. Accepted it. But never before had she cared for a newborn. Never before had she taken in a child who truly had no other family. Already she'd begun to think ahead with dread and unease to the day Molly would leave. If she somehow knew when the end was coming, she believed that somehow she could pace herself, protect herself, keep a piece of her heart held back.

Unbelievably, according to Kim the authorities had zero leads into who Molly's parents were. It was as if they had dropped her off at the church, then vanished. Most troubling about the situation was the lack of medical history. According to the doctor, Molly appeared to be in excellent health, but still, there was so much they didn't know. Had Molly's mother received prenatal care? Used drugs during the pregnancy? Had she smoked? Eaten right? Been exposed to any chemicals?

Even Molly's race was a mystery. Her eyes were, so far, a dark grayish blue, but the doctor said they would probably change to brown. Her complexion, creamy and smooth, looked darker than that of many Caucasian newborns. Her hair, brown and wavy, lay flat against her head like a lovely little cap. Kim thought Molly might be part Hispanic. Charlotte agreed she could be biracial. Half black, half white was her guess.

Not that she had anything to compare with, but it seemed to Charlotte that Molly's temperament was calm compared to other newborns—which was a good thing. She tolerated the girls passing her around, jostling her, arguing over who got to feed her next. She cried the most when she needed to nap, fretted softly when she was hungry or wet. Charlotte was usually up with her a couple of times every night.

Speaking of which. She yawned and looked at her watch. It wouldn't be long before Molly woke up for round one. Charlotte needed sleep. After checking to make sure she had two bottles ready, she tiptoed to her bed.

"Good night, Molly," she whispered as she crawled in between the sheets.

His home office illuminated only by the screen, Jock popped peanut M&Ms into his mouth with his left hand and worked his computer's mouse with his right. It was late. Past midnight. Fortunately, tomorrow was Saturday. Without any morning commitments, he could sleep in.

Though he wouldn't.

He would wake up before six, as he had every day the past week and a half, with Charlotte and the baby on his mind. Had they slept well? How many times had the baby woken up during the night? Did she take all of her bottle? Did she burp? It would take extreme discipline—he would have to force himself to dawdle and stall—to keep himself from arriving on Charlotte's doorstep before 10 a.m.

It was the baby that drew him . . . but it was Charlotte too.

Folks were talking. People in town and members at the church. He knew it. About how he was over at Tanglewood at least once every day—sometimes two or three times in a twenty-four-hour period. Jock was careful not to neglect his duties at the church—no one could say anything about how he was doing his job—but he could not deny to himself or to God how much his focus had shifted toward Charlotte and her girls, all of them. Not just the baby.

Was that a terrible thing?

He wasn't sure. He and Charlotte had had feelings for each other for more than a year. Both of them shyly, in roundabout moments, admitted such. But other than a few dates, neither of them had done much of anything about those feelings. Though he had held her hand once when they went to a movie, the two of them had not even kissed. Over the summer, their relationship had sort of stalled. Tentative, cautious, and uncomfortable with the ensuing gossip, Jock had let things get stuck on high center. Was it time to get unstuck?

Never before had he experienced such desire to *be with* someone as he felt toward Charlotte. Ever since he'd found the baby, his feelings of loneliness, his cravings for companionship—yes, for love—had grown until he felt nearly physically ill at the thought of not seeing her for an extended period of time. All day long, between feigned nonchalant trips to see for himself, he wondered what she was doing *now.*

Strange, the diversity of the people God chose to bring into each other's lives.

Seeing as how their pasts were nothing alike.

His teenage marriage had been little more than a joke. Thanks to his immaturity and selfishness, he and his wife had done little more than fight during the year and a half they were together. He'd had a few casual relationships after his marriage, but fearful of hurting another woman as he'd hurt his young wife, he'd not ever let himself get too close to anyone since.

Charlotte, on the other hand, spoke of her late husband often. From what Jock could tell, their marriage had been exceptionally good, marred only by their inability to have a child.

For years, Jock had believed God intended for him to be alone. He'd accepted that, and surprisingly had been fairly content. Not having a wife or children gave him tremendous freedom for ministry. He knew other ministers struggled with how to serve the church and be good husbands and fathers. How did one balance the two? Was his desire to be with Charlotte a sign that his devotion to God was less? But other ministers had wives, families—why not him?

God, You know I love You. All I want is to be Your servant. To love and serve Your people. Am I doing okay? Forgive me. Help me to focus on You and what

You would have for my life. If Charlotte and I are to be together, please let it be so.

After checking his e-mail, Jock went to Google.com. He typed in the words *abandoned baby,* then leaned back in his chair. It didn't take long for the Internet search engine to present him with pages and pages of references.

Specific information on Texas law was what he sought.

Chapter Nine

"Miz Lavada loves onions," said Kerilynn. She brought the take-out order to the table where Treasure waited with coffee and peach pie à la mode. "Thought I'd warn you. I put plenty on her burger. Fries are in this same sack, on top so they'll stay hot."

"Catsup?" asked Treasure.

"Nearly forgot. Here's napkins too." Kerilynn stuffed a wad into the sack.

"Thank you," said Treasure. The brown paper sack was already spotted with grease. "Mmm. Smells wonderful. How much I owe you?"

"Not a thing. Been meaning to get over and visit Miss Lavada. Ashamed of myself for not stopping by. You just take her this lunch and tell her I'm thinking about her. She's been in my prayers."

"You don't need to do that," Treasure protested.

"Yes, I do. Appease my guilt," said Kerilynn. "Last I heard, she may not get to go back home ever. Going backwards instead of forwards. Taking so many pain pills, she can't even get out of bed without help."

"What you gonna do?" Catfish had been eavesdropping from a nearby table. "Walk on Miz Lavada's back? Do some of that hocus-pocus on her?"

"Catfish!" Kerilynn shushed him. "People who do not know what they're talking about should keep their opinions to themselves."

"Shoot. Treasure knows I don't mean nothin.'" He wiped his mouth. "Massage. Hmm. Thur-pee what you call it? Time was when you didn't find that sort of thing outside of Dallas. Maybe Houston. Then again, whole world's changed."

Treasure felt every eye in the 'Round the Clock on her. That Catfish. He'd made jokes about her business since the day she'd announced her intentions, countering her best efforts to educate and interest Ruby Prairie citizens in the benefits of massage. She stood and put her hand on her hip.

"Do I look like some kind of a pervert to you? Miss Lavada's in pain. Her mobility is limited. She wants to go home, but she can't. Massage is an effective treatment for pain and stiffness. There's no hocus-pocus, and there's nothing improper about massage therapy. I'm trained to help people, and I intend to be a help to Miss Lavada."

"Oh, honey," Kerilynn soothed. "You don't pay him

no mind. His trouble is that he's got problems with regularity. Has had for *ye-ars*." She gave Treasure a clandestine wink. "You reckon massage therapy could help with that sort of thing?"

"Been known to," said Treasure. She flashed Catfish a condescending smile. "Catfish, honey, I'm running a special right now. Limited-time introductory offer. One-hour massage for $25. But for you, a special deal. Thirty minutes for $30. What time you want to come?" She plucked her sack from the table and marched out.

Leaving a café full of chuckles and one red-faced detractor behind.

"This has got to be one of the prettiest babies I have ever seen." Ginger Collins had brought over three warm-from-the-oven peanut butter pies. Assured that the dogs had been put up, she sat in Charlotte's living room holding Molly on her knees. "She is just per-fect."

The baby stared up at her with intent, dark eyes.

Charlotte had already given Molly her bath and dressed her in a pink-and-white footed sleeper. The color set off her dark skin and black hair. Thanks to the fancy baby lotion Alice had brought over, Molly smelled exactly like a fresh-baked pound cake. She lay relaxed on her back, her tiny hands curled into tight flower-bud fists.

"What's to become of her?" asked Ginger. "Will you get to keep her?"

"Kim says she has no intention of moving her from Tanglewood," said Charlotte, "as long as she's in the system."

At the sound of Charlotte's voice, Molly turned her head just the slightest bit.

"I'm here, Molly. I'm right here."

"She knows you," said Ginger, letting Molly grasp her little finger in a tiny pink fist. "Isn't that something. Two weeks old, and she already recognizes your voice. Of course, you're the only mother she knows. She's bonded with you."

"And I have with her," said Charlotte. "I never understood how mothers could interpret their babies' cries. You know—tell the difference between a hungry cry and a wet cry and a tired cry. I'm not sure I even believed it."

Ginger nodded. "But now you do."

"Yes, I'm starting to. Lots of things have surprised me. I always wanted a baby—longed for one. But even then, I had no idea a baby could be this much fun."

"Or this much work?"

"That too." Charlotte smiled. "I never did get a shower yesterday. I took one this morning, but no way did I have time to do my hair." She tugged on the short, fat braid at the base of her neck, smoothed back an escaped curl. "I don't think I've put on makeup once since Molly arrived. And forget White Shoulders. Spit-up is my new chosen scent."

"Amazing how much time a baby takes up," agreed Ginger.

"I'm not as efficient as I could be," said Charlotte. "We've spent lots of hours in the rocking chair."

"And not one minute of those hours was wasted," said Ginger. "Every second you spend with Molly in your arms is a treasure."

Charlotte was quiet for a long moment. "No one can tell you what it's like. My husband and I wanted a baby so badly. We tried for years, did all that infertility testing and procedures and such. He would have been a wonderful daddy. I don't know which one of us hurt worse when I lost the only baby we ever conceived."

"What will happen to Molly if they don't find her parents?" asked Ginger.

"I've asked Kim, but she's pretty vague."

"That doesn't seem right. I'd think you have a right to know."

"It's just the way it is when you're dealing with a government agency," said Charlotte. "I don't think Kim knows much that she's not telling. But Jock's been doing some research on the Internet. Seems that if her parents aren't found, there is a legal process where their parental rights would be terminated."

"And then?" asked Ginger.

"She could be adopted."

"That's wonderful news! You might get to keep her after all. I'm going to start praying for that. What a blessing this could all turn out to be. Don't you just love how the Lord works in such mysterious ways?"

Turning her back to Ginger, Charlotte got up to stoke the fire. Finally she put the poker in the rack and faced her friend. Her chin trembled, and hot tears filled her eyes.

"You're right. I could keep her. Foster families of babies are usually considered first as possible adoptive families when a baby is abandoned. But I love her too much already. I couldn't do that to her." She wiped her face on the sleeve of her faded chambray shirt.

"Oh, honey, what do you mean? You'd make a wonderful mother. You said yourself that you've already bonded with Molly. Is it the money? I know adoptions cost a lot. I read an article about it in *Reader's Digest*. But the church would help you. Lester and I would. No telling who else would chip in."

Molly began to squirm in Ginger's lap.

"It's not the money." Charlotte eased the baby from Ginger's knees and up into her arms. She put Molly up on her shoulder, took a seat in the rocking chair, and began to gently stroke the infant's back as she rocked.

"What, then?" Ginger scooted to the edge of the sofa.

"She deserves to have what every child needs," said Charlotte.

"Which is?"

"Something I can't give her. Molly deserves to grow up in a two-parent family. Sure, I could raise her. Honestly, I don't think I could feel more like her mother if I'd given birth to her myself. But Molly will either return to her birth mother or go to a family with a mother *and* a father."

"Oh, honey."

94

"My dad and I were so close. I can't imagine what it would have been like not having him. I won't deprive Molly of having a daddy," said Charlotte.

Molly had gone to sleep. She made little sucking sounds as she dozed against Charlotte's ear.

"You've made up your mind," said Ginger.

"I have."

"Sugar, only the Lord knows how your heart can bear what you do."

"When I opened this home, I knew girls would come and girls would go," said Charlotte. "I admit, it's different with Molly, because I know she'll likely be adopted. The other girls already have families—troubled, broken families, sure, but still they have families of their own. Molly has no one.

"But I feel the same way about her as I do the other girls. I promised myself on the day every one of the girls arrived that I would love and care for them as if they were going to be with me forever. What kind of a place would Tanglewood be—what kind of a mother would I be—if I held back from giving them total love and acceptance, just so it wouldn't be so hard for me? When Molly leaves, if my heart breaks, then I'll know that I've done what was the right thing."

"I admire you," said Ginger. "And, honey, it's plain to me that God has put you in exactly the place where you need to be. These girls are so blessed. It's got to be because of Him that you can do this." She wiped at her eyes. "No other way that you could."

"You can say that again."

Enough. Charlotte did not want pity. Nor admiration. Not even from Ginger. She smiled, blew her nose, then shifted Molly from her shoulder to the crook of her arm.

"Did I tell you the latest thing those girls pulled? We keep running out of towels. I couldn't figure out what was happening to them. Well, yesterday I found a stash of eight mildewed towels in the bottom of Maggie and Sharita's closet. Seems they found it too much trouble to bring them downstairs and put them in the laundry."

"Those two." Ginger shook her head. "Hard to believe you've still got all the girls you started with— not counting Beth."

"It is," agreed Charlotte. "Except for Sharita, none of them were supposed to be here for more than six months. I haven't told anyone, but I found out yesterday that Nikki and Vikki are leaving as soon as school lets out for the Christmas holidays. Their mother has finished her cancer treatments. Kim thinks she's strong enough to take them, and their grandmother will be there to help."

"They'll be so excited," said Ginger. "But I can't imagine Tanglewood without those two little scamps. What about the others? Will you have them over Christmas?"

"Sharita'll go home for a short visit. How long she stays depends upon how much she attracts the attention of the gangs in their neighborhood."

"I can't imagine what her parents have been

through," said Ginger. "Losing a son, then sending off their daughter."

"It was the only way they felt they could keep her safe. She may well stay at Tanglewood until she graduates from high school."

"What about Donna and Maggie?"

"Maggie's mom's prison term is up in February. There was no documented abuse or neglect, so there's no reason she can't get Maggie back. Kim says she's been working on her G.E.D.

"As for Donna—I don't know what's going to happen with her. Her dad's been off the oil rig for a month now. He's supposed to take Donna back to live with him, but Kim says he keeps stalling. Claims he needs more time to get settled first."

"Does Donna know that?" asked Ginger.

"No," said Charlotte. "She'd be terribly upset if she did. She counts the days till she can live with her dad again. I still can't figure out a man taking a job that keeps him from home for six months at a time when he has a teenage daughter with no one to care for her while he's gone."

"Has to be the money," said Ginger.

"That's what Donna says."

"Wonder why he's taking so long to come get her now that he's back?"

"Kim suspects he's got a girlfriend."

"Goodness," said Ginger. "The messes these folks go and get themselves in."

"Want to hear some good news?" asked Charlotte.

"Please."

"Beth'll be home in five days. Her school takes a break for most of December. She won't have to go back until after the first of January."

"That's wonderful news," said Ginger. "I can't wait to see her."

Everyone in Ruby Prairie would be wanting to know how Beth liked her school. Charlotte hoped they didn't overwhelm the girl. She'd been through a lot— and she was still only sixteen.

Beth had been pregnant when she arrived at Tanglewood. Unbelievably, not even Beth knew at the time. Kirby, who now lived with Treasure and Jasper, was the father. He and Beth had met at a shelter in Dallas before either one of them had even heard of Ruby Prairie.

What a scandal all of that had been, thought Charlotte, looking back. Folks in town had sure carried on. Even so, the premature birth and death of their baby had broken everyone's heart, and the town rallied behind Beth and Charlotte and even Kirby. Shortly after, the young couple had broken off their relationship. Without the baby to keep them together, they were just two teenagers with little in common. And Beth's admission into Wings of Gold, a prep school for disadvantaged students, had been an answer to Charlotte's prayers for God's hand to be upon Beth's life.

It was unbelievable how things had worked out.

And in less than a week, Beth would be back.

Chapter Ten

S almon patties and french fries.

The aroma of New Energy's lunch greeted Treasure when she arrived to see Miss Lavada. Recalling past experiences at less well-run nursing homes, Treasure did not think the fishy smell offensive in the least.

Just a bit strong.

What made New Energy unusual—aside from its name—was that the home was owned and operated not by a corporation or private owner, but by the town of Ruby Prairie. According to Mayor Kerilynn, citizen volunteers were the only thing that kept the forty-bed facility running. Volunteers raised the major funds, kept up the grounds, provided maintenance and repairs, and, during the growing season, donated bushel baskets of scrubbed produce from their fruit trees and garden patches so the residents could have a break from all that canned food.

The nursing home's reputation was so good that, except during the winter months when pneumonia and flu drove up the mortality rate, families generally had to endure a waiting period to get their loved ones in.

Treasure had visited New Energy just a month earlier, when Lighted Way took its turn hosting the monthly birthday party. She and Ginger and Kerilynn and Nomie had served German chocolate cake and strawberry punch to a grand gathering of eighteen ladies and five brave, cake-craving men.

Rose Ann Eden greeted Treasure in the hallway just outside Miss Lavada's room.

"How's she doing?" asked Treasure.

"Not a good day. Refused breakfast. Won't take her pills. Tried to slap the nurse's aide for attempting to get her into the bath."

"Miss Lavada?"

"She's not herself. Going downhill, I'm afraid. We see it a lot. Someone her age takes a fall, has some surgery, or just gets sick and has to spend time in the hospital. When they're out of their familiar environment, they get confused. It's like they were so fragile they were barely hanging on before, and then something happens and they get tipped to the other side."

"Poor thing," said Treasure. "Being in such a state, she may not let me touch her. I don't know if she'll remember who I am."

"What's in the sack?" asked Rose Ann.

"One of Kerilynn's cheeseburgers."

"Onions?" asked Rose Ann.

"Extra."

Rose Ann grinned. "Those should sweeten the offer, if not your patient's breath. Could be just what the doctor ordered." She motioned toward Miss Lavada's half-closed door. "Hope you're quick on your feet— she's got quite the left swing."

Treasure eased open the door. Miss Lavada lay on

top of the covers of her neatly made bed. The head had been raised, as had one side rail. Miss Lavada was dressed in a navy blue shirtwaist, stockings, and black pumps. She was holding a hairbrush in one hand, the *Penny Saver* shopping circular in the other.

"Hello," Treasure called. "Miss Lavada? How are you? May I come in?" Not waiting for an answer, she pulled up a chair and took a seat next to the bed.

Miss Lavada struggled to rise up a bit more and peered over her glasses. "I don't know anything about the dew. Haven't been out of this room in more than a year. Who are you?"

"I'm Treasure Jones. From church. I've brought you some lunch." Treasure raised the sack to nose level.

Miss Lavada sniffed.

Treasure heard the old woman's stomach growl. Taking that as a positive sign, she opened the sack and spread her 'Round the Clock offering on Miss Lavada's bed table. Thoughtfully, Kerilynn had cut the sandwich in half. Treasure arranged the cheeseburger, salty french fries, and a neat little puddle of catsup, then moved to pour a fresh glass of water from the room's bedside pitcher.

"Is there anything else you need?" she asked.

Miss Lavada didn't answer. She couldn't. Her mouth was already full.

Jock began his day on his knees. *Lord, use me today. Give me wisdom and strength to serve You. Bless my efforts. Forgive my failings. Guide my steps. Please,*

please make Your way plain for my life.

In his too-quiet house, over instant oatmeal and a tall glass of orange juice, Jock's thoughts went to Tanglewood and to Charlotte.

He had expected Charlotte to be thrilled at the Internet information he'd uncovered about the adoptability of abandoned children. Instead, when he told her that once parental rights had been terminated, Molly could be adopted, Charlotte's eyes had teared.

"That's wonderful," she had said. "I suspected it would be something like that. Molly will go to a good family. She deserves that."

"No," he'd protested. "This means we, I mean *you*, can keep her. You don't have to give her up."

Her dismissal of his expectations that Molly would live permanently at Tanglewood had stunned him.

It shouldn't have.

He could see them.

A married couple. Young. Probably late twenties. Childless. Established, but just starting out. Eager for a family, unable to have children of their own.

Once the way was clear legally, it was the right thing for Molly to be given to someone like that. But how would Charlotte bear it? How would *he* bear it? He was at Tanglewood every day. It was probably his imagination, but it really seemed as though Molly recognized him. Charlotte thought she did.

"See how she kicks her feet when she hears you? When she sees your face?" Charlotte had said just yesterday. "You're glad to see Jock, aren't you, baby girl?"

When Jock held Molly on his knees and she wrapped her little fist around his thumb, his heart swelled with an aching tenderness. Yet even as he held her and played with her and talked to her, never far away was the impending, implosive wound that her leaving would inflict.

He couldn't help but wonder, what would his child have been like? The one who never lived to rest in his arms? Would he have had a daughter or a son? Would the child have grown up to favor him or to look more like his nineteen-year-old bride? That unexpected, unwanted—at least by him—baby would be more than twenty years old today if her mother had carried her to term. At the time, he hadn't grieved the loss—a fact that he now could not comprehend.

As for this child he'd held for so many hours in his arms?

There was no doubt.

When she was gone, he would grieve.

If only Charlotte would reconsider.

Jock rinsed out his glass and his bowl. He stood at the sink, looking at the bare trees in his yard. What about Charlotte? His feelings for her? Spending so much time at Tanglewood had created a growing domestic ease between the two of them that their half-dozen dates had not come close to accomplishing.

Not that they'd had a real date in weeks. Since Molly's arrival, lasagna dinners at Joe's had been replaced with rowdy evening meals he helped Charlotte prepare for the girls. The two of them had developed a dancing, domestic dinnertime routine. One or the other cuddled Molly and directed traffic while the other poured milk, fetched napkins and second helpings, and wiped up spills.

Instead of going to the occasional movie, as they'd done in the past, after supper and homework he and Charlotte took turns rocking Molly in front of a fire he built every evening. Once the girls had all gone to sleep, the house would be quiet, and he and Charlotte would talk and talk, late into the night.

About the girls.

The school.

The church.

And the town.

And while he wanted to talk about *them,* they mostly talked about Molly.

Jock always knew when it was time to go home. Charlotte would begin to yawn. Their rocking chairs would slow. They'd both begin to laugh at things that weren't all that funny and to have trouble thinking of their words. He would look at his watch. Molly would take her bottle, burp, and fall asleep in a pair of arms. Charlotte would say something about putting her to bed.

Last night he had been holding Molly when the time came to leave. Instead of taking her from his arms, Charlotte led him to her bedroom where Molly's crib was set up. The cozy room, cluttered with baby paraphernalia, was softly lit by the shaded hurricane lamp on the table next to Charlotte's unmade bed.

Jock tiptoed across the room, holding Molly to his chest. Gently, he laid her down. Once she was settled into her soft nest, he and Charlotte stood shoulder to shoulder watching her sleep.

Finally, Jock bent and kissed Molly on the forehead. Charlotte turned off the lamp.

And Jock returned to his home—to toss and turn and finally dream of a time when he wouldn't have to leave Tanglewood.

When he and Charlotte wouldn't have to say good-bye.

Kerilynn took off her coat, hung it up in Tanglewood's entry hall closet, and made herself at home. "I brought over banana pecan muffins. Fresh from the oven. You got any breakfast coffee left?"

Charlotte carefully closed the door to her bedroom and turned on the baby monitor. The girls were at school and Molly, up since five thirty, had gone down for a morning nap.

"Muffins?" She peeked into the sack Kerilynn had set on the table. "You are too sweet. I'll put a fresh pot on."

"You had breakfast?" asked Kerilynn.

"Uh. No. I don't think I did. And I just realized I'm starving."

"You've lost weight. What are you now? A size six?"

"I don't know." Charlotte tugged on her overalls. "These are a ten."

Kerilynn snorted. "Ten? Well, no wonder there's room for you and a small family in there. Listen to me. You've got to eat better. And get more rest. Don't take care of yourself, you'll get down and not be any good to anybody. You taking vitamins?"

"Every day. All natural. Treasure keeps me stocked."

"At least that's something."

"I'm fine," said Charlotte. "Just busy is all."

"Keeping late nights?"

"Molly is a night owl," said Charlotte.

"Evidently so is Pastor Jock. Word at the 'Round the Clock is that he's over here most every night to near midnight."

"He was here last night," allowed Charlotte.

"And the three nights before that," said Kerilynn.

"Jock's crazy about Molly," said Charlotte. "He wants to be with her. That's all."

"Honey," said Kerilynn, "you are a smart girl, but in some ways you are as thick as a brick. That man wants to be with you. I know he's concerned about that baby, but you and him have been seeing each other for months now. All this started way before Molly came along."

"I don't think so," said Charlotte. "For a while, I believed there might be a future for Jock and me. But lately, we don't talk about us. We talk about the baby. We're friends. Maybe someday we'll be more. But for

106

now, it's all about Molly. He's at Tanglewood so he can spend time with her."

"Any word on how long you'll have her?"

"Still no trace of her parents. Kim says in a couple of weeks they'll begin legal proceedings to terminate parental rights. Once that's done, she'll be available for adoption. My guess is that she'll be here until sometime in March. Maybe April."

"And you haven't changed your mind?"

Charlotte and Kerilynn had had this conversation before.

"I can't keep her. I want to." Charlotte twisted the paper napkin in her hands. "You have no idea how much I want to. But she needs more. More than just me and a houseful of girls who will come and go. She's a healthy infant. There's no telling how many young, infertile couples will want her."

Charlotte sipped from her mug. "I've prayed for her every day since she arrived. I prayed for her birth parents. Still do. But now I've been praying for the mother and daddy who will become her adoptive parents. I believe with all my heart that God has the perfect family for her."

Kerilynn placed her hand over Charlotte's. "You are one of the most unselfish people I know. I don't know how you do it."

"Yes, you do," said Charlotte. "You know exactly how. I'll get through this the same way you got through losing your husband when your boys were so young. I'll get through it the way all people of faith do. My heart will break, and I'll want to quit. I will think I cannot possibly go on. But I will."

Kerilynn got up to pour more coffee. "Honey," she said quietly, "how does Jock handle the thought of Molly leaving?"

"He thinks I should adopt her. It's going to be really hard for him when she's gone. I think finding Molly brought up a lot of his old stuff. You know. His marriage. His wife losing their baby. The divorce."

"How long was he married?"

"Less than two years."

"Jock's a good man."

"He is. He's a good man who cares deeply about the little baby asleep in her crib."

Chapter Eleven

You want to do what to me?" Miss Lavada's high-pitched voice prompted folks in the hall to peek into her room so as to make sure the poor woman was okay.

She'd finished her lunch, and as far as Treasure could tell up until then, the two of them had been getting along like old pals. They'd chatted about the new carpeting Miss Lavada planned to lay in her house, discussed how long she'd lived in Ruby Prairie, and talked about what a good pecan crop the year had

108

brought in. Miss Lavada even remembered how Treasure had once brought the Tanglewood girls over to her house to rake up leaves.

"Yes," Miss Lavada recalled. "That was very kind of those girls to do that for me. Now what did you say your name was again, dear?"

"Treasure Jones."

"And what is it again you want from me?"

Treasure cleared away the wrappings from Miss Lavada's lunch. "I'd like to give you a massage. A back rub."

"No, ma'am. I am not getting into the bathtub," said Miss Lavada.

She struggled to sit up higher in the bed, likely, Treasure surmised, for better leverage should she need to fend off unwanted bathers and such. But even that bit of movement caused her to wince. Bless her heart.

"Miss Lavada. Settle down," soothed Treasure. "You misunderstood. No bath. I'm here to make your *back* feel better. We're not going anywhere near the bathtub. Promise. Come on, honey. Listen to me. I've brought some thick lotion. See? Doesn't that smell nice?"

"So how did it go?" Jasper asked that night.

He and Treasure, along with Kirby, had just sat down to Crock-Pot beef stew.

"She let me rub her feet," said Treasure. "But I didn't get past her ankles before she made me stop. Said she had somewhere important to be and didn't have time for such nonsense as that."

"You giving up?" asked Kirby. He reached for a pickle.

"No. I'll go back tomorrow. With another cheeseburger." She grinned. "Who knows. Maybe I'll get as far as her knees."

Jasper sipped his iced tea. "Saw Charlotte at the grocery store today," he said. "She had that baby with her. Sitting up in her carrier in the cart like a little queen."

"She's a doll," agreed Treasure.

"Charlotte told me Beth was coming in next week. She'll be home at Tanglewood until after the first of the year."

Kirby stirred his stew.

Treasure and Jasper exchanged looks. When they had invited Kirby to come live with them, he'd packed his bags and, as far as they could tell, never looked back. Since coming to live in Ruby Prairie, Kirby had behaved himself surprisingly well. Treasure and Jasper had expected some acting out, maybe even outright rebellion.

There were lots of issues, and some Ruby Prairie folks questioned the wisdom of their inviting him to come stay. At sixty-three and fifty-five, the two of them were pretty old to be parenting a teen. Then there was the racial issue. They'd wondered to each other if the arrangement would work out, but felt that they had to give it a try—that the unwanted, unloved sixteen-year-old deserved some kind of a chance.

So far things had gone well, though Kirby didn't

110

talk a lot about how he was feeling. Best they could tell, he'd made only a couple of friends and had shown no interest in any Ruby Prairie girl.

Treasure saw no point in beating around the bush. "How's it going to be, Kirby? Seeing Beth?"

"I don't know. All right, I guess."

"Y'all had any communication since she left?"

"I e-mailed her. Once. But she didn't write back."

"Maybe she didn't get it," said Jasper.

"Maybe," said Kirby.

"You still have feelings for her?" asked Treasure.

Kirby met her eyes. "I used to. Not so much anymore. We talked before she left. We're just friends now. That's all. Can I have some more stew?"

Jock realized, as he dialed the number from the phone in his church office, that it had been more than two months since his last conversation with his friend and mentor, Grady Moore. How had he let so much time slide?

They'd met twenty years before, when Grady, thirty years old and working as a hospital chaplain, discovered Jock—emptied of everything he thought he'd ever had—on his knees in the chapel. Upstairs, his mother was dying, and Jock, who'd not read more than five chapters—maybe five verses—in the Bible his whole life nor sat in a pew more than a dozen times ever, had given it all up to God.

That day Grady took Jock, who had no idea what a person was to do next, to breakfast at Denny's. Later

111

he'd baptized him, bought him a Bible, and hooked him up with a church. They'd been friends ever since.

"Grady. Jock here. How are you?"

They chatted for ten minutes before Grady cut into Jock's recounting of the latest goings-on in Ruby Prairie and at Lighted Way.

"Enough about all that. You've gone to circling, man. Something's going on. Tell me, do you need to come see me?"

Jock considered it. Though Grady lived in Dallas, over an hour's drive away, perhaps he did need some time with his old friend.

"You sure I won't be imposing?"

"Of course not. Plan on spending the night. We'll catch up."

That night, after Grady's wife and son had gone to bed, leaving the two of them in the dim quietness of Grady's home office, Jock poured it out.

He leaned forward and put his elbows on his knees, cupping a mug of hot decaf in his hands. "Grady, I'm tired of being alone. For the past twenty years I've believed I was meant to devote myself to my work—and I was fine with that. But lately it's not enough. I'm lonely. I rattle around in my house like a pecan in a coffee can. Nothing feels right."

"Is this about Charlotte?"

"Yes. I think so. But maybe it's more than just her. Honestly, it's getting embarrassing. Folks are talking. Every spare minute I'm at Tanglewood. If I can't think of a legitimate excuse to go over there, I make one up.

I tell myself that since she's taken in the baby, she needs my help, but the truth is that I just want to be in the same room with her."

"We've talked about this before. Charlotte's a wonderful woman. You've been seeing her for months now. Just sounds to me like it's time you do something about your relationship. Do you want to marry her?"

"Yes. I do. I think I do. But is it the right thing? I'm distracted. Not nearly as focused on the church, on my sermons, on the needs of the congregation. Remember that big speech I gave the hiring committee at Lighted Way when they were considering calling me to be their pastor? They weren't sure about a single pastor. I had the best spiel. Told them that unlike a married man, I wouldn't be distracted by a wife and children. I could stay with the sick at the hospital as long as I was needed, devote myself to study and to prayer. I would be more available to them. They could call on me day or night."

"Did you mean it?" asked Grady.

"Of course."

"What's changed?"

"Nothing. Everything. Me." Jock shook his head.

"Your love for God changed?"

"No. Of course not."

"How about your feelings for Lighted Way? You've been there what—five years?"

"Going on six."

"Time enough to learn your congregation's warts."

"And for them to learn mine." Jock leaned back in

his chair. "I love Lighted Way. The members there are flawed people who make messes and bicker and complain and carry on, and yet lavish love on me and one another in ways that stun me. Which is why I'm at such a loss to explain why, instead of feeling satisfied with my life as it is, I feel restless and out of sorts. I don't understand why, after years of contentment—fulfillment—I'm so out of sorts."

"I'd say you've fallen in love. Which is not a bad thing. Do you think I'm a good pastor?"

"Of course."

"How is it that I'm able to be married and serve, but you think *you* have to choose?" asked Grady.

"It's not the same thing. You've been married your entire ministry. I haven't. I'm accustomed to devoting everything I have to my work. I'm forty-one years old. I don't know if I can manage both a wife and the church. If I choose to be with Charlotte, am I choosing to take back from God what I've already promised Him?"

"Are you?"

"I don't know."

"I can't answer for you," said Grady. "I believe you're a good pastor single, and you'd be a good pastor married. Being attracted to Charlotte isn't wrong. Wanting a wife isn't wrong. Your life is God's. I know over the years you've asked Him to guide your steps. Perhaps He's guided your steps to Tanglewood."

"Or perhaps I've taken a detour," said Jock.

"You've prayed?"

"Of course."

"But you don't have peace about this."

"No. I wish I did, but no. I don't have peace."

"Then wait until you do."

Beth. Back at Tanglewood. Sleeping in her old room. Sitting at her place at the table. Tonight. Charlotte put fresh sheets on Beth's bed and tucked Hershey's Kisses under the pillow before smoothing the quilt.

Had she really been gone six months? Even though they talked on the phone at least once a week, Charlotte missed her terribly. Kim was picking her up at the airport and bringing her to Tanglewood. To see her and hug her and make sure *she was really all right* was the one thing Charlotte wanted for Christmas.

Word was out, and on this, the first day of December, Charlotte wasn't the only Ruby Prairie citizen excited about Beth's homecoming. A crew of Lighted Way men were coming bright and early to bring her a tree and to hang outside lights from Tanglewood's eaves. Ruby Prairie Culture Club members were coming to help Charlotte and the girls decorate inside. How special it would be, everyone agreed, to have Tanglewood decked out for Christmas when Kim drove up with our Beth.

"Girls, it's time to wake up."

Charlotte went first to Nikki and Vikki's upstairs room. Though Vikki's bed had the covers disturbed, the two of them, as alike as a pair of new shoes, snuggled knees touching knees in Nikki's single bed. Most nights the twins started out in their own beds. Many nights they ended up together. Neither girl knew that in a week and a half they'd be going back home to live with their mother and grandmother. Tomorrow, she would tell them.

The sisters were the first girls to come to live at Tanglewood when Charlotte opened her home over a year ago. She remembered standing on the porch on that September day, holding her breath, shaking with excitement and anxiety, watching the twins tumble out of Kim's car. How she had grown to love those two.

How she would miss them.

Charlotte reached under the covers to tickle Nikki's toe. "Remember? It's Saturday. We're putting up the Christmas tree today."

She went to Maggie and Sharita's room next. Red hair spread out over the pillow, Maggie lay uncovered, the legs of the sweatpants she favored for sleeping pulled up over her knees. Sharita, in her twin bed on the other side of the room, was covered up under her quilt and three extra blankets.

"Good morning," Charlotte called. "Time to wake up. Cinnamon rolls and hot chocolate for breakfast."

"Mmumf," grunted Maggie, not moving.

Sharita's head popped out of the covers. "Can we have bacon?"

Donna, because she was the oldest, got one of the upstairs bedrooms to herself. Charlotte knocked on the closed door, then opened it a crack. "Donna. Are

116

you up? Can I come in?"

"You can come in. I'm awake." Donna was sitting on her already-made bed, polishing her fingernails.

"That's pretty," said Charlotte. She sat down on the end of the bed. "I like the pink sparkles. Are you excited about Beth coming home tonight?"

"Sort of," said Donna. "I mean, yeah. I can't wait to see her. But what if it's weird? What if she's changed? What if I don't know what to say to her?"

"I imagine it will be weird, and she probably has changed," said Charlotte. "But I don't think the weirdness will last long, and change isn't always so bad."

Donna didn't answer. She blew on her nails.

"All right," said Charlotte. "Breakfast in ten. Can you get dressed and help me pour milk?"

Before going to Miss Lavada's room, Treasure hunted the halls until she found Rose Ann passing out meds.

"Two aides called in sick," explained Rose Ann at the med cart. "I'm already running twenty minutes late." She placed two pills in the slot of her med crusher and began to pound them into powder.

"Bless your heart," said Treasure. "Quick question, won't take a minute. I passed Miss Lavada's house. What's that For Sale sign doing out in her yard?"

"Isn't that the saddest sight?" Rose Ann shook her head and stirred the pulverized pills into a tiny cup of applesauce. "I just hate it, but her kids were here yesterday morning. After seeing the shape she's in, they decided it was best to go ahead and get things settled."

"What are you talking about?" asked Treasure.

"Miss Lavada doesn't know it, but she's not going back to her house. It wouldn't be safe. She's staying here permanently."

"Because she can't get around?"

"No way she could take care of herself," said Rose Ann. "Her mind's not so clear, and her mobility's not improving. She can't get out of bed without help. How in the world would she be able to manage alone at home? It's a shame, but that fall got the best of her. By the way, she let you do anything for her yet?"

"We're making progress," said Treasure. "I'm hoping today she'll let me give her at least a massage in the chair. Her children shouldn't be so hasty. I still think I can get her up and moving. But I need more time."

"Long as they haven't sold her house, nothing's been done that can't be undone." Rose Ann held a tiny cup of cough syrup to the lips of a man in a wheelchair.

"Charlie," she said, "once we get this medicine down you, let's take a nap. You ready to go to bed?"

Charlie looked up and shot Rose Ann a lecherous grin. He chugged the cough medicine, then reached around to pat her on the rear. "Sure, honey. Anytime you are."

Rose Ann, well practiced, sidestepped his grope, shooting Treasure a look over his head. The two of them struggled not to burst out laughing. Rose Ann plopped a kiss on the top of Charlie's head, then called for an aide to assist her Romeo to his room.

Grinning, Treasure headed down the hall to Miss Lavada's room. New Energy was not a bad place, but if Miss Lavada had a chance of going back home, even for a short while, she wanted to give it her best try.

"Miss Lavada," she said at the woman's bedside. "Today is the day you and I get better acquainted. *Much* better acquainted."

Chapter Twelve

"W here we going with this?" Catfish Martin stood in the bed of his mud-slung tan pickup truck, the first of half a dozen vehicles gathering in Tanglewood's gravel driveway. His flushed face was nearly obscured by the lush green tree he hoisted, ready to hand down to Lighted Way deacons Gabe Eden and Dr. Lee Ross.

Nikki and Vikki, Donna, Sharita, and Maggie, just up from the breakfast table, still breathing cinnamon and chocolate, swarmed Catfish's truck. Donna, up for more hot milk, had seen it pull up into the driveway and alerted the other girls. The morning was cold and gray, but without taking time to put on their coats, they'd tumbled down the back kitchen steps to get a look at the tree.

Charlotte, carrying a hastily bundled baby Molly, trailed down the driveway behind them. "Wow! What a gorgeous tree," she said. "Since it's going in the living room, we need to take it in through the front door."

"Hope you've got a stand," said Catfish.

"It's on the porch."

Nikki and Vikki hopped up and down.

Donna grinned from ear to ear.

"How come we don't got artificial?" said Maggie.

"Stand back, honey," Dr. Ross urged Sharita, almost at Catfish's feet. "Don't want y'all getting hurt when he tosses that thing down."

"I think we should put it in our room," said Maggie.

"No way," said Nikki.

"That's a really big tree," said Donna. "It's beautiful."

"Ten feet," said Catfish. Having tossed his burden, he joined the rest of them on the ground. "Prettiest tree on my place."

"Good morning!" Alice and Nomie, having parked in the street, were making their way up the sidewalk.

"Girls," directed Charlotte when she saw her friends struggling with oversized plastic totes, "the ladies need some help. Donna. Maggie."

"What's in here?" asked Maggie, reaching for one of the totes.

"New ornaments," said Alice.

"Bought on sale at Sam's Club on the 26th of last

120

year," said Nomie. "Donated by the Ruby Prairie Culture Club."

Behind them, Charlotte saw Kerilynn's baby blue station wagon pull up and park behind Alice's van.

From their house on the other side of Charlotte's, Lester and Ginger appeared. Both of them carried staple guns.

"Your outside lights down from the attic?" asked Ginger.

"Where's your ladder, sugar?" asked Lester.

"Got it," said Pastor Jock. He carried the ladder under one arm.

"Where did you come from?" asked Charlotte. She hadn't seen his truck.

"Just got here." He set the ladder down. "Parked around the side." His eyes went to Molly. "How's the princess?" he asked. "Ready for her first Christmas tree?"

Charlotte knew he wanted to hold her. He always did. Without any prompting, she placed the baby in his arms. Then she secured Molly's little cap and tucked an escaped, bootied foot back into the blanket.

Jock planted a kiss on Molly's cheek. "How'd she sleep?" he asked.

"Only up once," said Charlotte.

"What a good girl you are, letting Mommy—I mean Charlotte—sleep," Jock cooed.

Molly kicked and squirmed.

Jock flashed Charlotte a smile.

One she returned.

121

"Well, if y'all don't look like the perfect little family," Kerilynn interrupted. "Standing there like something off the front of a Christmas card. Why, Pastor, Molly even favors you. Got your eyes. Your dark hair. Pretty as a picture, all y'all are. Fact, I've got my camera in the car. Catfish"—she looked around for her brother—"get my Polaroid out from behind the front seat. Box of film back there too.

"Hold it right there. Don't move. This is good. We need to get some pictures of all this going on. Charlotte, move in a little toward Pastor Jock. Hold the baby down just a little where we can see her face. Now y'all smile. Oh, that's good."

Charlotte eased her tired self into the tub. For the first time all day she had a moment to herself. Since this morning, Tanglewood had teemed with helpful Ruby Prairie folks. Thanks to their spirited Yuletide efforts, the house, porch, and yard were all decked out in red and green. The tree was up and decorated. Garlands circled the posts on the porch. Icicle lights hung from the eaves. An on-sale nativity scene, minus a missing wise man, graced the mantel.

What fun the day had been. She'd watched the girls as, breathless and pink cheeked, they handed lights up the ladder to Lester, helped Catfish put the tree in the stand, and tossed tinsel in great glistening globs on the tree.

Time had gotten away from everyone until straight up at noon, when Treasure, Jasper, and Kirby arrived bearing chili and stew, cheese and crackers, iced tea and fresh apple cakes. Suddenly hungry, everyone stopped long enough to perch on the porch and have a bite to eat.

It was now nearly five o'clock. The girls were all next door at Ginger's house.

"We're going to bake cookies and watch that new Christmas special on PBS," she had explained. "Lester'll walk 'em back home about ten."

Treasure was the only extra person still in the house. She'd sent Jasper and Kirby to take care of a list of errands without her. After a few minutes resting with mugs of tea in front of the living room fire, Treasure insisted Charlotte relax in a hot bath.

"Go on. I'll watch Molly. Take your time. If Jasper gets back before you're out, don't worry about it. He'll wait. When's the last time you had a nice long soak?"

Too long. This was nice. Charlotte leaned back in the tub, laying her head on a rolled-up towel. Lulled by the hot water and the scent of the lavender salts she'd added, she closed her eyes in sleep for just a moment. Delicious.

But then the phone rang, prompting her to jerk awake.

Only two rings?

Treasure must have gotten it.

Was it Kim? With word about Beth's flight? Surely not a cancellation or a delay. Her plane was scheduled to land in Dallas at eight tonight, putting her at Tanglewood sometime after ten.

"Who was that on the phone?" Charlotte padded into the living room, wrapped in a robe, her hair in a towel. "Was it Kim?"

"Nope. Pastor Jock. He wanted to know if you'd like to have dinner with him. I told him I was sure you would, but that he should give you an hour to get ready."

Charlotte shot her a look.

"What?" Treasure shot her one back. "You've got to eat. Wouldn't you have said yes if you'd answered the phone yourself?"

Charlotte laughed. "Yes. No. Oh, I'm not sure. But since you've gone and accepted this invitation on my behalf, you mind dressing Molly while I get ready?"

"Molly looks fine," said Treasure. "But if it's not too early, I can go ahead and put her in a sleeper so she'll be ready for bed."

"But if Jock's taking us to dinner—" Charlotte began.

"Not *us,* honey," said Treasure. "You. I'm taking Molly home with me. You, missy, are taking tonight off. No discussion. You need to get out. Without this baby. Every mother needs some time to herself. Now go put on something pretty for the pastor. Me and Molly here have our own plans, don't we, baby girl?"

Jock, stalling till time to go to Tanglewood, sat down in his living room and turned on *Wheel of Fortune* in time to see a woman in a tight blue sweater win a minivan. He plucked Kerilynn's photo from the lamp table next to his chair and held its sticky edges in his hand. He turned it over and saw she'd written the date on the back. Who knew they even still made Polaroid film?

Jock studied the image. Charlotte. Baby Molly. And him. Kerilynn was right. They did look like a family, albeit one with squinting, slightly-older-than-normal parents. Why couldn't they be one? No reason, according to his friend Grady.

A family.

It would start with him and Charlotte.

And include the Tanglewood girls.

But not Molly. With no sign of her biological parents, termination of their rights was already in the works. Adoption would be close behind. When Molly left to go to her new family, would he and Charlotte ever see her again? Jock didn't know how that worked. Would they cut off all contact? Maybe experts thought it better if a baby got an all-fresh start.

Could be they were right.

But it would be so hard for Charlotte.

He thought about the day they'd spent together. With Molly snuggled into a blue canvas baby pack strapped onto her chest, Charlotte had been right in the middle of all the holiday goings-on at Tanglewood. Dressed in jeans and a green sweater, her curly hair flying all over her face, she'd strung lights, wrapped garlands, and directed traffic—all with grace and good humor. He'd watched as she refereed fights, soothed hurt feelings, encouraged, cajoled, and dealt gentle, firm discipline when it was needed. If ever there was a woman meant to mother a houseful of children, it was Charlotte.

Which sort of made her and the Tanglewood girls a package deal.

If he proposed to Charlotte, if—he dared think about the possibility—they married, would he make a good father to this ready-made family? Could he, after living alone all these years, adjust to a houseful of females? Charlotte made him feel as if he could. Since Molly's arrival and his embarrassingly frequent visits to Tanglewood, she'd routinely included him in whatever she and her crew were involved with at the time.

Which most of the time was fine, though he did get embarrassed the other day when he arrived to find Charlotte folding three loads of clean laundry piled on the dining table. Not thinking, he'd set in to help.

Oh, my.

All those bras. Panties too. Keeping his eyes decidedly up, he'd tried to nonchalantly pluck washrags, towels, and jeans—safe things—from the pile, but since Charlotte was out of fabric softener, there'd been lots of static cling. Despite his best efforts, he'd found himself more than once peeling sparking nylon undies from his chest.

Alone in his house, he reddened at the memory.

Forget about being a good father—would he be a good husband?

Old thoughts of his past marital failure rose to the

surface like scum on a pond. He'd been selfish, immature, and unfaithful. He'd not felt compassion, concern, or even—this was hard to admit—love for Ashley, his teenage bride.

Did he love Charlotte?

Yes. He did.

The physical reaction to this realization took his breath. It felt the same as when, last Saturday, spending the afternoon with Lighted Way youth, he'd gotten the wind knocked out of him by a plus-size seventh-grade girl during a game of what was supposed to be noncontact touch football. He'd lain on the ground, sweating, fighting panic, knowing that if he could wait it out without going totally nuts, his breath would come back sooner rather than later.

The thought of having to *do something* about his feelings for Charlotte, of having to somehow wedge the relationship off of high center where it had for the past months been stuck, made him grin on the outside, groan on the inside.

Change. That's what it was. That's what it would take. This meandering along, waiting for something to develop, had gone on long enough. Either he wanted a life with Charlotte or he didn't.

What a surprise it was to find himself in love. Maybe the fact was a given to everyone else in Ruby Prairie, but it was absolutely a shock to him. What had begun as sincere friendship had grown into a longing to be with Charlotte every day for the rest of his life. Grady had asked him, "What is it about Charlotte that appeals to you? What about her attracts you, makes you want to be with her?"

"She's a good Christian woman," he'd said. "Good morals. Strong convictions. Family oriented."

"And . . . ?"

"Honest. Resourceful. Helpful."

"Sounds like you're describing a model member of my son's scout troop," Grady teased. "I suppose she's also kind to animals and good to the elderly?"

Jock grinned, leaned back in his chair, and threw open his arms. "Okay, okay. What do you want to know? She's cute. Charlotte's really cute."

"What's she look like?"

Grady was enjoying this.

"All right. She's medium tall. Five foot eight. Thin—not like as in frail, but small. Well, not *small* exactly. I guess she's medium. Yeah. Medium."

"She has a nice build," said Grady.

Jock willed himself not to give Grady the pleasure of a blush. "Yes," he said, "you could say Charlotte has a nice build. How do they put it? Height proportionate to weight?"

"I see," said Grady. "She's physically fit. Good quality in a wife. What else?"

Grady was not giving up.

Jock coughed, then acquiesced. "She's got blue eyes. Fair skin. Hair that's sort of reddish blonde. Curly. It's pretty long. Past here." He touched his shoulder. "Sometimes she pulls it back. Mostly she wears it down."

128

"Nice dresser?"

"I don't know. She wears overalls a lot. Jeans. Sweat suits sometimes. She wears dresses to Sunday church."

"So she's pretty casual," said Grady. "A low-maintenance gal. That's good. What about her personality? Is she a talker or more quiet?"

"Both," said Jock. "She's easy to talk to. Sometimes, I think, she holds stuff in. I can't always read her. With all those girls, she's usually got a million things on her mind. She's independent. Doesn't like to ask for help."

Grady shook his head. "That independence thing isn't going to go away. Could give the two of you some problems."

"Could," said Jock.

"Nothing that can't be worked through," said Grady. "And as far as you not being able to read her—quit trying. Ask. Talk about stuff."

"Yes, Daddy," said Jock.

"Communicate."

"Yes, sir."

"And for goodness' sake," Grady concluded with a grin, "take the woman someplace nice for dinner."

Chapter Thirteen

When Jock rang the bell at Tanglewood, he was surprised to see Treasure open the door.

"Hello, Pastor," she said, giving him a bosomy hug. "Come on in out of the cold. Don't you look nice. And, lands, you smell good too. Why, I could eat you with a spoon. What is that cologne you've got on?"

"Aramis." He'd worn it since high school.

"Christmas is almost here; I'll have to get some for Jasper. Reckon they sell it at the Wal-Mart? Now you just come on in and sit down for a minute. I'll let Charlotte know you're here. You want something to drink?"

"Thanks, no. I'm fine. Where's Molly?"

"Asleep in her bed. Wore out from all these Christmas goings-on. But she'll be awake and calling for her supper any minute."

"The tree looks great. Catfish outdid himself," said Jock. He declined Treasure's offer of a seat.

"That man is full of surprises," agreed Treasure. " 'Scuse me. I think I hear the little lady waking up."

"You want me to—?"

"Nah. Stay put. I'll get her," said Treasure. "Probably needs to be changed."

As if he hadn't done that many times. He'd changed,

bathed, fed, and burped Molly—gotten pretty good at it, if he did say so himself.

Jock studied his nails.

Whatever.

He was standing, gazing at the ten-foot pine beauty adorned with dozens of ornaments, when Charlotte came into the living room. He turned to face her.

Wow. She looked nothing like the jean-clad woman who, only a few hours before, had been right in the middle of all the decorating frenzy. Slim black slacks. Mid-heel black boots. A baby blue sweater that made evident the rarely seen but highly appreciated . . . uh . . . *build* she usually obscured beneath overalls, sweats, and baggy shirts. Her hair was different too. Pretty. She'd pulled it back into a loose bun kind of a thing. Soft curls framed her face. She had on lipstick.

And she smelled good too.

Jock tried not to stare. Or at least to keep his stare focused above Charlotte's neck. "Nice boots," he finally said. "I bet they're warm."

"They are." Charlotte studied her boots for a second, then glanced back at the tree. "It does look pretty."

Thankfully, she seemed oblivious to the fact that his attention had completely abandoned the tree.

"Wait till you see how it looks when I plug in the lights." Charlotte knelt to get the cord. "Won't Beth love it?"

"She will. I bet you can't wait to see her."

"You have no idea. I'm so glad you called," said Charlotte. "The girls are at Ginger and Lester's. Treasure's going home. If I'd been here by myself just waiting, I'd have gone crazy. This will help pass the time."

"Glad to be of service," said Jock. "Are you hungry?"

"Starving."

"This little girl's hungry too," interrupted Treasure, coming into the room with Molly in her arms. "But she wanted to see her pastor before she had her dinner."

"Hi there, sweetie. Did you have a big day?" Jock gooed and cooed at the baby, touched her cheek with his thumb, then planted a kiss on her starfish fist.

Molly's face wrinkled into what looked to be a grin but according to the books he'd read was probably gas.

Jock turned to Charlotte. "Your van unlocked?" he asked. "I'll put the car seat in my truck. When Molly is done with her dinner, we'll be ready to go have ours."

"Oh," stammered Charlotte. "I thought . . . Molly isn't going."

"She's not?"

"I'm babysitting," said Treasure quickly.

"I'm sorry," said Charlotte.

"What do you mean, sorry?" said Jock, vaguely aware that he'd said something wrong. "That's fine. I just expected it would be the three of us."

"Treasure said—" Charlotte started. Her face pinked. "I think I misunderstood. There's no reason for us not to take Molly." She set her purse down in the rocking chair next to the tree and reached to take the baby from Treasure's arms. "Just give me a couple of minutes to feed her and get her dressed."

Jock looked at Treasure. His palms had grown moist.

"Nonsense," said Treasure. "Pastor, I've been telling Charlotte here that she needs to take care of herself. Have some grown-up fun. She's not been apart from this baby for a minute. Be good for her to get out. Be good for both of you."

"Of course. I absolutely agree," said Jock with genuine, if overstated, enthusiasm.

It *would* be nice to spend time alone with Charlotte. Just the two of them. He'd prayed about this evening, about the turn he wanted his relationship with Charlotte to take.

And folks sometimes doubted that God answers prayers.

"You're sure?" asked Charlotte.

"Absolutely."

"We can take her."

"No. Really. Let's not."

The ride to Joe's was mostly silent.

"You warm enough?" Jock asked.

"I'm fine." Charlotte looked out the window.

"Supposed to rain tomorrow," said Jock.

"That's what I heard."

"Joe's okay?"

"Of course."

Lord, the evening's just begun, but I don't believe we're having much fun, Jock informed God. He steered his truck into the crowded parking lot of Ruby Prairie's only real restaurant, found a spot, shifted into park, and turned the key. *I could use a little assistance here.*

Charlotte got out.

Uh. Lord, I'll take whatever You've got.

It had been way too long, decided Jock, since his and Charlotte's last date. Right there in the parking lot of Joe's it came to him. Enough. No more stalling like a skittish dental patient needing to schedule a root canal. Though the thought terrified him, he knew. Before the night was over, he would tell Charlotte exactly how he felt.

That okay with You, Lord?

He believed that it was.

Treasure had Molly fed, bathed, and dressed in her footed sleeper when Jasper and Kirby came in the back door of Tanglewood to pick the two of them up.

"How'd it go?" asked Jasper.

"You don't want to know," said Treasure. "That girl. She has got some kind of an attitude going on."

"What do you mean?" asked Kirby. He snagged a Little Debbie snack cake from the open box on top of the fridge.

"She was fine this afternoon," said Jasper. "Everything looks so nice. She unhappy with the tree? The outside lights?"

"Not that," said Treasure. She handed Molly over to him, then slung the baby's diaper bag over her shoulder. "I meant her and Jock. She's as skittish as a deer on a golf course. And him? He's so nervous he don't hardly know what he's saying."

"Sounds like love," said Jasper.

Kirby grinned.

Jasper reached for a cake.

Treasure nodded. "Of course it is. Those two've been in love going on six months now. I don't know what's wrong with them, aside from the fact that the lady of this house needs to get her hormones checked. I've been telling her she ought to switch her milk to soy."

She snatched the Little Debbie box out of her husband's hands. "What's with y'all eating up all Charlotte's snacks? These things are nothing but sugar and fat. Look at all the chemicals they put in." She turned the box over. Nothing came out.

"Rats," she said with a grin. "I was hoping there was one left."

Charlotte picked at her lasagna, the specialty of the house.

"You no like?" asked Joe, who'd come out of the kitchen to make his rounds. "Too much spice?"

"No," said Charlotte. "It's very good." She was glad they were seated at the back. Entering the restaurant, the two of them had been greeted by a generous showing of grins and hellos, followed by a wave of poorly concealed whispers.

"You not hungry then," said Joe. "Something more to drink?"

"Everything's great, Joe," said Jock.

"I bring you more bread."

"Really. We're fine here," said Jock.

And Charlotte supposed that they were. Once they'd gotten to the restaurant and been seated, conversation had gotten easier. There was just so much going on. With Beth expected in only a few hours, she wasn't herself. How else to explain her hurt feelings? Was it so bad that Jock had wanted Molly to come with them? He tried to spend every possible minute with the baby. Why should tonight be any different?

She fiddled with her napkin. That Treasure. This was her fault. She'd led her to believe this was a real date. Encouraged her to dress up. She should have worn jeans.

How long had it been since the last time Jock asked her out? Charlotte counted back. At least two months. Though being a forty-two-year-old widow was not how she'd pictured her life playing out, she'd had the blessing of a good husband for twenty years. Now she was blessed to have a good friend. Which meant that little Molly, at least while she lived at Tanglewood, was blessed to have a male figure in her life who loved her so much.

She smiled at Jock. My, my. Blessings all around.

It was nice of him to have invited her out to dinner even if it wasn't a date. She needed to quit thinking so much. Relax. Be grateful for the pleasure of a delicious meal in the company of a warm friend.

Forgive me for being ungrateful, Lord. Thank You.

"You look nice tonight," said Jock. He'd finished his pasta, but instead of leaning back, he moved his plate to the side and hunched forward in the booth.

"Thanks. So do you."

The fine-gauge black sweater he wore over his pressed khakis did look nice. As did his dark eyes and his in-need-of-a-trim curls. She liked longish hair on a man.

Jock motioned toward her plate. "You're finished?"

"Yes."

He looked at his watch. "It's early. Want to go for a drive?"

After pulling out of the restaurant parking lot, it didn't take long to leave Ruby Prairie. Outside the city limits, Jock steered the truck toward Ella Louise. Tall pine trees lined both sides of the two-lane road, obscuring all but a ribbon of moonless black sky. They didn't meet a single car.

"Remember the first time we made this drive?" asked Jock.

"We were on our way to get Beth. The night she ran away."

"What a wild goose chase that was."

"Seems like longer ago than it was," said Charlotte.

"We hardly knew each other back then."

The lights of Ella Louise were visible, though still several miles ahead. Jock slowed the truck, then signaled to turn.

"What are you doing?"

"This is a roadside park. Nobody uses it. See— there's a little clearing off to the left. Sometimes I park here just for the quiet. Is that okay?"

Charlotte shivered when Jock killed the engine.

"Cold?"

"A little."

He reached behind the seat. "This help?" He unfolded a quilt and moved close enough to lay it across her lap. When he did, his cold fingers brushed against hers. At first he drew back, but then, after only a second of hesitation, he took her right hand in both of his.

Charlotte's heart sped.

"It's so hard for us to get a chance to talk," he said. "We're never alone." He coughed. "Even at Joe's, it's like the whole town's watching and listening in. There's so much on my mind. Some things I want to say."

Charlotte could not look him in the eye. They'd had this conversation before. As he'd pointed out again and again, a child could be raised by a single parent and do really well. Love counted for so much.

Though he'd voiced agreement in principle to Molly's need for a two-parent family, Charlotte knew he'd not accepted the fact that soon the baby would be leaving, and neither of them would see her again. She'd told him how hard this was for her. Did he have to go there again?

"Jock, this isn't easy for me," she said.

"Please. Just let me say what I have to say."

Charlotte steeled herself.

"We've known each other for more than a year. I feel like we're more than friends, but I need to know. Do you have feelings for me?"

"I—" She began. What? Where was he going with this?

"Because I have feelings for you." He didn't let her answer. "I have for a long time, but I got stuck. I don't know why. Maybe stuff in my past. I got so used to being alone, to believing that's where I was supposed to be, that I closed off the thought that I could ever be with a woman again. I don't believe that anymore. I'm tired of being stuck. I want to be with you."

Charlotte's nose began to run.

"We're not sixteen," he continued. "Though I sort of feel like it right now." He let go of her hand to wipe his own on his pant leg. "You may think this is out of the blue, but it's not. I want to make a commitment to you. I'm ready to be together."

Charlotte tucked her hands under the quilt and wished for a tissue. She had to say something. Jock was waiting. In the silence of the truck she could hear how quickly his nervous breath came.

"Charlotte. This isn't the most romantic setting in the world. I should have planned something special. But this isn't spur-of-the-moment. I've thought about it and prayed about it, and I'm sure. The honest truth is that I want us to get married. Not sometime off in the distant future. Now. Well, not like tonight, but soon. Really soon."

Charlotte began to cry. What was there to say? Her

139

heart was touched and broken both by what he'd said and what he'd not said.

He wanted to marry her. But he hadn't breathed one word about love.

She sniffed and wiped her nose on the back of her hand, then tucked it back under the quilt.

Why was she surprised?

Jock had it all figured out. He'd given it thought. He would marry her, and they could keep Molly.

A kinder man she'd never met.

Chapter Fourteen

The ringing of Charlotte's cell phone broke the silence inside the cab of Jock's truck.

"Goodness. That might be Kim. I hope Beth's plane's not delayed."

Charlotte tossed aside the quilt, groped for the purse at her feet, and fumbled inside it for her phone. Wallet. Lotion. Keys. Where was that phone?

"It *is* Kim," Charlotte announced, glancing at the caller ID. "You're where? . . . That's great! . . . Really? Wonderful! . . . Yes. Tell Beth we can't wait to see her. . . . All right. Drive safely. Bye."

She turned to Jock. "Beth caught a little bit earlier flight. She and Kim are on their way. Should be in Ruby Prairie in an hour."

"Great," said Jock.

"I'm so excited," said Charlotte. She kept her purse in her lap and her phone in her hand. "Beth sounds so good when I talk to her, but I need to see her in person to believe that she's really doing all right."

"I bet she's thriving," said Jock. He made no move to start the truck. "I'm glad they're getting in early. But continuing our conversation . . ."

Charlotte didn't acknowledge his words. She found a tissue in her purse and blew her nose. "Jock—I'm sorry. We've got to get back. I'm calling Ginger to tell her to get the girls ready. They should all be at the house when Beth arrives. I'm not sure what to do about Molly. You think we should go get her? Treasure was going to keep her overnight, but since Beth's getting in early, I sort of want to go get her now."

"I can take you to Tanglewood and then go get Molly," said Jock. "But, Charlotte, we're not twenty minutes from Ruby Prairie. Kim won't be there for an hour. Let's finish our talk. Who knows when we'll have another chance?"

Charlotte shook her head. "I'm sorry, Jock. I can't think of anything except Beth getting home."

"Can you at least give me an idea what you're feeling?" asked Jock. "About what I said?"

"What I'm feeling is that I want you to take me back to Tanglewood," said Charlotte. She sat up straight in the seat so as not to see his expression. "Can we please go?"

Finally, he turned the key.

141

• • •

Except for her hair being longer and her having gained maybe five pounds, Beth looked the same. From the kitchen, where she was arranging cookies on a plate, Charlotte could see through the breakfast area and into the living room where all six girls chattered away.

Beth was on the couch, Nikki and Vikki on either side of her. Vikki cuddled so close she was practically in Beth's lap—except that it was already occupied by Visa. Charlotte didn't have to be closer to know Visa was purring like a motor. Sprawled on the floor in a half circle at Beth's feet were Donna, Sharita, and Maggie.

"Do you like it up there?" asked Donna.

"Pretty much. Except that it's cold. There's snow everywhere. On the weekends they take us to this mountain. Some kids ski. Not me. They have snow-boards. They're fun, but I'm not very good."

"Are your teachers nice?" asked Nikki.

"Most of them, except for my biology teacher. He's a grump. And you should see how high he wears his pants." Moving the cat from her lap, Beth stood up and demonstrated. "And his belly is out to here."

The girls fell over laughing.

"Any cute boys?" asked Sharita.

"Yeah," said Maggie. "You got a boyfriend?"

"Not really."

"Charlotte does," said Nikki in a lower voice.

"Pastor Jock," said Sharita.

"He comes over here *all* the time," said Maggie.

● ● ●

"So. How was your dinner last night?" asked Treasure. She'd shown up at Tanglewood at eight o'clock.

"It was good." Charlotte got up to pour them both more coffee to go with their shared late breakfast of scrambled eggs and buttered wheat toast. Molly was down for a nap. The girls were still upstairs asleep—all of them piled up in Beth's room. Even after she'd shooed them upstairs, Charlotte had heard happy thumps, bumps, and giggles well into the early morning hours.

"Jock had chicken fettuccini. I had lasagna."

Treasure looked at her. "Y'all get a chance to talk?"

Charlotte stalled at the counter, her back to her friend. How did Treasure always know? "You won't believe what he asked me."

"Try me."

"He asked if I had feelings for him." Charlotte sat down and pushed her plate to the side. "Then he told me he thought we should get married."

Treasure set her mug down hard. "It's about time. That's wonderful! I wasn't sure that lead-footed man had it in him. Did you set the date?"

"Set the date? You think I said yes?"

"Didn't you?"

"No!"

"Are you crazy, girl? That man is for keeps."

"You're wrong, Treasure. It's Molly he wants. Not me."

"What are you talking about?"

143

"Jock can't bear the thought of Molly leaving. If we get married we could adopt her. He's got it all figured out." Charlotte wiped at her eyes. Wished them dry. Why tears now?

"Is that what he said?"

"Not in so many words, but it's the truth."

Treasure put her hand on Charlotte's arm. "Honey. That man is in love with you. He's been in love with you since way before Molly came. I don't believe none of this is about Molly."

"Last night . . ." Charlotte swallowed. "He didn't say a word about love."

"Shoot, is that all? That don't mean nothing," said Treasure. "Some men won't never say that word. It hangs in their throat like a piece of chicken bone. You got to see what a man's feeling by the way he acts.

"I'm telling you, Charlotte, that man loves you. When he's over here—which is, from where I'm sitting, most all the time—he can't take his eyes offa you. He's a good man. A honorable man. You need to take him at his word."

"Which is?"

"That he wants to marry you. You didn't go and turn him down, did you?"

"Not exactly."

"Thank the Lord. You two just got to talk some more. Straighten this out. Sugar, this is a blessed day." Treasure looked at her watch. "You do yourself some studying on what I've said. Put it to prayer. I've got to run out to New Energy and see Miss Lavada. Me and her's got us a little work to do."

The nursing home was decked out in splendid Christmas finery. Three artificial trees stood sentry in the lobby, each one decorated with a different theme. Treasure studied them one by one.

On one side of the outside door was the patriotic tree, decorated, she assumed, in honor of the many veterans who resided at New Energy. It was hung with red, white, and blue balls and miniature American flags.

Back in the corner was a tree put together by the nursing staff. It was hung with glitter-glued medicine cups and needle-less syringes filled with red and green colored water.

Near the entrance to the south hall was the most traditional tree of the trio. It was hung with construction paper chains, red and green satin balls, and candy canes.

"Pretty, aren't they?" said Nomie Jenkins, on her way out. "Me and Alice just finished up with the decorations in the dining room. Take a look at the tube-sock snowmen Alice made. Cutest things you ever saw."

"I'll make sure I do," said Treasure. "You seen Miss Lavada this morning?"

"I have. She's looking better. Up in her wheelchair. Mind seems clearer. I hear you've been giving her back rubs."

"Massage therapy," said Treasure. "To ease her pain and increase her mobility. Not unusual for an elderly person to get confused when they're in the bed for a period of time. I'm hoping getting her up and moving will clear her head."

"I never knew giving a person a back rub could do that."

"It's not just back rubs. It's massage. Therapy," corrected Treasure. *Don't get your panties in a wad,* she told herself. *She doesn't mean anything by it. Ignorance. That's all this is.*

"I've had training, you know. And been at this a good thirty years. People came from all over to get massage therapy at my clinic in Oklahoma. I've helped athletes, pregnant women, nurses who've hurt their backs lifting patients, even children."

"Really? I had no idea," said Nomie. "I mean, I've seen the sign at Lila's shop, but I didn't exactly know what it was you were doing shut off in that back room of hers."

"No secret. And no hocus-pocus about it," said Treasure. "Massage therapy is a science. An art too, but it's all based on solid science."

Nomie looked at her watch. "Got to run. But God bless you for what you're doing for Miss Lavada. Those back rubs are sure doing her a world of good."

Treasure found Miss Lavada in the dining room drinking a cup of coffee and eating an oatmeal cookie. "There you are. You're already up. That's wonderful. Feeling better?"

Miss Lavada shot her a suspicious, sideways look.

Treasure sat down so as to be eye level with the woman. "It's me, Treasure Jones. Remember? I'm the lady what works on your back."

"Yes. Of course you are." Miss Lavada smiled. "I'm sorry, dear. I didn't recognize you. Can I offer you a cup of coffee?"

"No, thank you. I'm fine."

"Did you bring your little girl with you today?" asked Miss Lavada.

"What little girl is that?"

"The one with the baby."

"Sugar, you're just a wee bit mixed up." Treasure put her hand on Miss Lavada's arm. "You must be thinking about someone else. My little girls are all grown up. They live a long ways off."

"No. There was a little girl." Miss Lavada put her cookie down and wiped her mouth on her paper napkin. "I saw her. She was colored like you. Pretty little thing. Where has she gone with that little baby?"

No sense in arguing. Obviously Miss Lavada's mind wasn't yet completely clear. Treasure put her finger to her brow and feigned recall. "Oh. That girl. She's gone back home."

"With her baby?" asked Miss Lavada. Her brow was furrowed, and her watery blue eyes displayed genuine concern.

"Yes. She took her baby home. They're both fine."

"You're sure they made it home all right?"

"Yes. They're both okay."

This seemed to satisfy. Miss Lavada took a last sip of coffee from her cup, then moved her purple-veined hands to her lap, concentrating on smoothing the folds of her blue-belted dress. "Now what did you say you needed from me, dear?"

"How about we go down to the therapy room?" suggested Treasure. "Do a little work. Then you can show me the Christmas trees in the lobby. That sound like a good plan?"

Miss Lavada allowed that it did.

Like an old person with creaky bones, Tanglewood's eaves and rafters shimmied and groaned in the quiet of the night. Charlotte, in Hawaiian print flannel pajamas, was making her bedtime rounds, Mavis and Jasmine at her heels. The dogs' tails wagged in slow circles, and their toenails clicked against the hardwood floor.

Maggie and Sharita's room was the first on the right at the top of the stairs. Charlotte opened the door, then stood and watched them sleep. Those girls. They slept in twin beds in a room that was forever a chaotic mess. Both of them snored. They were competitive and sometimes cranky as cornered crawfish with each other, yet had been best friends since the day they met.

Charlotte swallowed. Maggie was going to miss Sharita during the two weeks she'd be home with her parents for Christmas break. Then, come February, Maggie's mom would be out of jail and Sharita would be the one left behind. Once Maggie went back to live with her mom, it was unlikely the girls would ever see each other again. To the two of them, February seemed like a long way off. Charlotte knew just how quickly the time would pass.

She left their jumbled quarters and moved to stand in the doorway of Donna's room. The books on Donna's shelves were arranged by height. Her desk chair was pushed in just right. Even the quilt covering the sleeping girl remained straight. What Donna wished for most was an orderly life, one that included just her and her dad in a home of their own. In his last letter, he'd promised he'd pick her up on Christmas Eve and the two of them would spend the whole week together.

Lord, please let him show up when he says he will. Please, oh, please, just let him come.

While it was difficult to pray for him to take Donna back to live with him permanently, Charlotte sent a request up for just that. She believed with all her heart that, barring abuse, it was best for children to live with their real parents—even parents whose pasts were marred by flawed and foolish choices.

That fact was what made running Tanglewood so difficult. Folks all the time asked Charlotte how she could do it. Within the next few months several of the girls would be gone. Possibly all of them.

It will break my heart, she told those who asked. I'll cry and I'll mourn and I'll probably feel like I'm going to die. But I won't. I'll get up and make up the beds and get ready for Kim to bring more girls.

At least that was the plan.

In the next room, Charlotte moved to tuck the quilt over Beth's uncovered foot. For months after coming to Tanglewood Beth had slept curled up in a tight little fetal ball. Tonight she slept on her back, arms flayed out at her sides, mouth open, hair fanned out over her pillow. It was so, so good to have her back at Tanglewood. Charlotte planned to cherish every day of her month-long break from school.

While the other girls had hopes of eventually going back home to their biological families, Beth, with her severely mentally ill mother, did not. It was Wings of Gold that promised a future for her. A future that included long-term mentoring and free college if she did well.

Softly, Charlotte closed the door of Beth's room.

It was the sight of Nikki and Vikki sleeping together in Nikki's twin bed that caused Charlotte's throat to lump. The twins were leaving tomorrow. The two of them had taught her so much about how to mother girls. She loved their knobby knees and elbows, their spontaneous hugs, their little-girls-on-the-brink-of-adolescence innocence.

Tomorrow.

How would she manage to say good-bye? How would it feel to stand on the porch and wave as Kim drove them away?

Help me, Lord. Give me the strength. Forgive my selfishness. Make me glad. I don't feel very glad tonight.

Charlotte looked at her watch. Nearly one. She headed down the stairs to catch a few hours' sleep. "You coming, girls?" she called to the dogs.

Mavis and Jasmine stood at the top of the landing and watched her descend.

"Come on." She patted her leg.

The pair cocked their heads but didn't move. Instead of joining her downstairs, they turned and clicked their way down to Nikki and Vikki's room, where they nudged the door open and disappeared.

Charlotte waited a moment, then climbed back up the stairs and looked into the room. The dogs were settled, curled up at the foot of the twins' shared bed.

Chapter Fifteen

Juggling a mug of coffee and the stack of mail he'd retrieved from the post office while whistling the first line of "What a Friend We Have in Jesus," Jock unlocked his office, turned on the lights, and punched the telephone answering machine for messages.

Beep. "Pastor, Catfish here. Got a bone to pick with you about Sunday's sermon. All that business about turning the other cheek is well and good. Then again, some folks mighta gone and got the wrong idea. That concerns me. This is America. Lord's who give us the right to keep and bear arms. Be good if you could

151

clear that up come Sunday." *Click.*

Jock smiled. Anytime something didn't strike Catfish as well to the right of center, he could be counted on to squawk. At least a person always knew where he stood with Catfish. Man didn't talk about folks behind their backs. No sirree. He said whatever came to his mind straight to a person's face.

Or at least to his answering machine.

Bee-eep. "Pastor Jock, this is Nomie Jenkins. Forgot to let you know I'm in need of two more Sunday school student workbooks for my sixth-grade class. Could you order those for me? I'd so appreciate it. See you Sunday. Bye now."

Jock made himself a note.

Beep. "Jock. Grady here. How you doing, man? Give me a call. Want to know how things are going with Charlotte. Later."

Things were going okay with Charlotte. The conversation in the truck hadn't ended quite the way he'd hoped, but that was because of Kim's phone call. Charlotte hadn't had a chance to tell him how she felt. But he knew. There was a future for them. He was sure of it.

Christmas was coming.

The perfect time.

He planned to buy a ring.

On Nikki and Vikki's last morning, Charlotte woke up with nausea and a splitting headache. She'd wanted to make their favorite breakfast, banana pancakes and

152

bacon, but she could barely manage cold cereal, and there was not enough milk to go around.

Then Kim called. "I'm so sorry. My car's broken down. Mechanic said it'll be fixed in about three hours. I hate to ask, but instead of my coming to Tanglewood, could you bring the girls to me?"

"Sure, Kim. I mean, I guess I could," said Charlotte.

She glanced at Nikki and Vikki. Excited, but on edge, they had both stopped chewing and were listening to every word.

"It's okay. Everything's fine," she mouthed.

But it wasn't. The day was falling apart. Saying good-bye to the twins in some parking lot was not the way she'd wanted their time with her to end.

"Hold on," she told Kim. "Let me get a piece of paper for directions."

Shoot. The pen wouldn't write. Molly, balanced in the crook of her arm, began to cry. A wave of nausea hit, and Charlotte broke out in a cold sweat.

"Just a minute. . . . Yes . . . I got it. And you want them there at noon. Okay."

Charlotte hung up and took deep breaths, trying to hold it together.

"What's the matter?" asked Donna.

"Nothing. Everything's fine. Oh, honey, I'm sorry; I just don't feel well."

Donna took Molly. "She's wet."

"Would you change her? Please?"

Bracing herself against the counter, Charlotte gave in and phoned Treasure. "Are you busy?"

153

"Not too. What's the matter?"

Charlotte started to cry.

"It's those girls, isn't it? I knew you weren't doing as well 'bout them leaving as you let on," said Treasure. "This gonna be a rough day. Sugar, you want me to come over?"

"I'm sorry." Charlotte sniffed. "I hate to ask. But I really do need you. It's not just the girls leaving. I mean, it is." Her head pounded. "I don't feel well. I might be getting sick. Molly is fussy. There's still stuff to do. Somebody's got to take the twins to Dallas."

"Dallas? Whatever for? And what kind of sick are you?" Treasure took charge. "You need Jasper to carry you to the doctor while I look after the girls? You want me to pick you up some medicine on my way over? Why in the world have they got to go to Dallas?"

"No. Yes. I don't know. Oh. Sorry. I've got to go."

"Oh-h. You're *that* kind of sick. Gotcha. Don't you worry, honey. Be right over with the Pepto."

In the end, Charlotte did stand and wave good-bye to the twins from her porch. Treasure was there. Jock. Lester and Ginger Collins. And Mayor Kerilynn.

Charlotte hugged Nikki and Vikki and kissed the tops of their heads, then leaned against Jock's shoulder and tried not to cry when the two of them, wearing matching yellow backpacks and pink plastic sunglasses—good-bye gifts chosen by the Tanglewood girls—scampered down the front steps and dashed down the sidewalk to get into Jasper's truck.

Just before they got in, they turned and waved.

"Bye, Charlotte!" called Vikki.

"Bye, everybody," called Nikki.

"Later gators!" yelled Sharita.

"Drive safe," called Treasure.

The door of the truck slammed. Across the street, a dog barked. Donna, Beth, Sharita, and Maggie stood shoulder to shoulder, leaning over the porch railings. No one spoke as they watched the girls climb in, buckle their seat belts, and slam the truck door. Finally Jasper cranked the vehicle, pulled out, and within seconds drove out of sight.

For a long time, no one on the porch moved. The wind picked up, and a swirl of dry leaves fell from the pair of live oak trees that grew in front of the house. Donna was crying. Beth too. Kerilynn wiped at her eyes. Lester coughed. Treasure busied herself with the baby in her arms.

Charlotte felt like a chunk of her heart had been ripped away. Visa rubbed against her ankles. When Jock tightened his grip on her shoulder, she could feel his arm tremble.

How could it be that Nikki and Vikki were really gone?

Predictably, it was Maggie who broke the spell. With great aplomb, she harked up a big wad of spit, then leaned over the railing and hurled it to the ground.

"Gross!" yelped Sharita. "You got some on me."

"Did not."

"It's not fair." Maggie wiped her mouth with the

back of her hand. "They get to go home and we don't. I hate it here."

"I'm going home for Christmas," said Sharita. "In four more days."

"I'm going too. On Christmas Eve. That's just one week from today," said Donna.

"And I'm stuck staying here at this dumb old place," said Maggie. She kicked at a porch post.

"It won't just be you. I'll be here till New Year's," said Beth.

Charlotte moved from Jock's side to gather the girls in her arms, then had to stop, stand very still, and take deep breaths to keep from throwing up. Could this day get any worse?

"Girls, y'all are coming with me and Lester," said Ginger. "We've got a surprise planned. Even Charlotte doesn't know what it is. We're going to load up in the van and make a trip to the Wal-Mart. Y'all done your Christmas shopping yet?"

"I don't have any money," whined Sharita.

"Me either," said Maggie.

"Yes, you do," said Lester. "Remember when you girls did all that work helping me and Ginger rake leaves?"

Charlotte remembered. The girls had thrown more leaves at each other than they had raked.

"We never did get around to paying you," said Lester. "Been feeling bad about that. Thought we'd settle up today."

"I'm hungry," said Maggie.

156

"We'll eat out," said Ginger. "They've got a real nice cafeteria right down from the Wal-Mart. Or we could go to McDonald's."

McDonald's? That clinched it. With the closest burger joint a good thirty minutes away, fast-food withdrawal was a common topic of conversation among the Tanglewood girls.

"Everybody inside," said Treasure. "Brush your hair and your teeth. Maggie, you need to change your shirt. Lester, y'all taking Charlotte's van?"

"It needs gas," said Charlotte between deep breaths.

"I'll go fill up," said Jock. "Charlotte, are you all right?"

"Fine," she lied. "Lester, Ginger, thank you so much. The girls needed something special to do today." Her eyes filled.

Treasure handed Molly off to Kerilynn. "Take this baby and put her down on a pallet in the living room. Charlotte, you need to be in bed, without Molly stirring in her crib next to you. Come on."

"I'll lie down once the girls are gone." Charlotte sat down at the table. "Maybe if I could have some tea."

Treasure put the water on to boil and offered to make some dry toast.

Charlotte shook her head. She knew it wouldn't go down.

The girls were finally downstairs and ready to go.

"Have a good time," Charlotte told them, without getting up. "Be sweet. Mind your manners."

When they were gone, the house got quiet and Char-

157

lotte slumped in her chair. Finally, she allowed herself to be led to her bedroom.

Treasure turned back the covers, helped her take off her shoes, and tucked the comforter around her. "Rest, baby. Just rest." She closed the blinds, tiptoed across the room, and pulled the door till it was almost, but not quite closed. "Call me if you need anything. I'll be here all day."

In the chilly, darkened room, Charlotte curled up on her side, tucking her fists under her chin. Which hurt worse—her pounding head, her cramping stomach, or her breaking heart? Nothing had prepared her for how difficult it would be to watch Nikki and Vikki leave. Every day for over a year, she'd been their stand-in mother. She'd made their breakfasts, brushed their hair, held their bony little bottoms on her knees even though they were too leggy to fit on her lap.

And now, just like that, they were gone.

Reunification. That's what Kim called it. Get children back with their families of origin. Always the goal.

Other foster parents did this. What was wrong with her? Fresh tears filled her eyes. She reached for a tissue on the nightstand.

Perhaps she wasn't cut out for this after all.

"Is she all right?" asked Jock. "I've never seen her like this." He'd started to follow Treasure into Charlotte's bedroom, but she'd stopped him with a look. Everything in him wanted to be right beside her. He hated

158

that she was in pain. Wanted to fix it. Surely there was *something* he could do.

"She will be," said Treasure. "Just something she's got to work through."

"You think she's got the flu?" asked Kerilynn.

"Nah. She don't have no fever. She might have a touch of virus. Give her some time to herself. Her body's just showing on the outside what she's feeling on the inside. Grief can make you feel sick."

"It sure can," said Kerilynn. "When my husband passed away I had chest pains. Went to my doctor. Figured on top of ever'thing else, I must be having a heart attack. Turned out wasn't one thing wrong with my ticker. Just stress. Still hurt though."

She wiped at her eyes and looked over at Molly, who lay on a blanket sucking her thumb in her sleep. "No way I could do it," said Kerilynn. "Take care of these children, then let them go."

"Charlotte's not superhuman. She's just like us," said Jock, his voice sounding sharp even to his own ears. "It's killing her right now that those girls are gone."

Charlotte's tender heart was what he was most attracted to. He felt an odd need to defend her.

"You're right, Pastor," said Kerilynn. "What I said didn't come out the way I meant it. No one could love these girls more than her. I just don't know how she can bear it, is all."

Treasure cut in. "Pastor, let's have prayer. For those two little girls what just left. For they mama and they

159

grandma. For the rest of this house. For Charlotte too."

Why, of course. He should have suggested it. After all, didn't he pray for Charlotte every day? For himself too. It was selfish, but he couldn't pry from his mind the thought that the day was coming soon when he'd have to say good-bye to Molly. How did a person get through something like that? As a pastor, he was supposed to know.

Some things they didn't teach you in seminary.

His thoughts went to Charlotte, asleep in the dark. *God be with her.* What else was there? Where else was there to go?

"Ladies." He swallowed. "Let's go to the Father right now."

Chapter Sixteen

Charlotte scribbled yet another item onto the bottom of her to-do list. One would think having two fewer children in the house would make everything easier. Not so. Nikki and Vikki were gone, but the needs of the other girls had swelled like yeast dough to fill the gaps in her schedule.

Schedule? That was a laugh.

On the morning that the twins left, Charlotte went to bed and stayed there for the rest of that day and all of the next, leaving her friends to care for Molly and the other girls. Finally, on the third day, she woke up ready to get up, get showered, and get moving.

While her throat still caught at the sight of Nikki and Vikki's empty room with its matching, made-up beds, and she still half expected to see them bounding toward her like two frisky colts, Charlotte was functioning. No. More than functioning. She was thinking ahead. Looking forward to Christmas. Hatching plans to make this holiday a good one.

Today was the last day of school before the holidays. Sharita's bags were packed and waiting at the bottom of the staircase. Kim was picking her up at Tanglewood and driving her south to Houston.

God, keep that girl safe, Charlotte prayed.

If her dad showed up as he'd promised, Donna would be leaving on Friday, Christmas Eve.

Lord, please help that man keep his word.

So. Though they would be few in number, Charlotte was determined Christmas at Tanglewood would be special. It would be just Charlotte, Maggie, Beth, and, of course, baby Molly. Since that didn't feel like nearly enough bodies to make for a festive day, Charlotte had invited Treasure, Jasper, and Kirby to spend Christmas Day, as well as Jock, Kerilynn, and Catfish.

Charlotte began a grocery list. What should she cook? Traditional, or something else? The thought of doing a turkey was a bit much. Mexican might be good. Or maybe a couple of different kinds of soup. Served with some crackers. Corn bread. Cheese. A raw veggie tray.

Kerilynn called. "Sugar, since you've got so much to do, me and Treasure have done decided we don't want you worrying none about food."

"That's too much trouble," said Charlotte.

"Nonsense. Won't be any trouble at all."

Charlotte twirled the phone cord around her wrist. Word of her cranberry sauce fiasco had gotten around. So had tales of her many other culinary gaffes.

"If you insist."

"I do."

"Fine. I'll have the table set and plenty of iced tea made."

"Wonderful. Can't wait. We'll be there bright and early on Christmas Day." Kerilynn hung up.

Relieved, Charlotte scratched cooking details right off her list.

Rose Ann caught Treasure in the hallway at New Energy. "Can you come into my office for a sec? Need to talk with you."

Sinking into a chair in the closet-sized office, Treasure braced herself for the worst. Despite Miss Lavada's progress, she figured somebody had complained. Or started some rumor.

"Residents' families are talking," said Rose Ann.

She knew it. Treasure looked at the floor. Rose Ann's rug sure needed cleaning.

"They've seen what you've done for Miss Lavada. How she's up and around now, probably even going home within the next few weeks. They're asking if you can work your magic on their loved ones."

What?

"Well, knock me over with a feather," said Treasure. She raised her chin. "I thought you were calling me in here 'cause somebody had complained. Honey, you know I don't do any magic. Just massage. I just set out to help ease Miss Lavada's pain and get her up and moving a bit. Anything beyond that's the Lord's doings."

"I realize that," said Rose Ann. "But up and moving, Miss Lavada's mind has cleared up."

"Except for that business with the colored girl and the baby," said Treasure. "She still talking about that?"

"Yes, there's some lingering confusion. I don't wonder at that. The woman *is* past eighty." Rose Ann leaned forward in her chair. "But back to you. Would you be interested in keeping regular hours here? Maybe being available for our residents a couple of mornings a week?"

"I think we could work that out," said Treasure. "Long as folks' families realize I'm no miracle worker."

"You have any written information I could give out?"

"Got some pamphlets that explain the basics of what massage therapy is about."

"Wonderful," said Rose Ann. "Bring them next time you come."

Treasure stood up to go. Miss Lavada would be waiting.

"One more thing," said Rose Ann. "Gabe's gone and

done something to his shoulder. Doctor says it's just a strain, but it's keeping him tossing and turning all night. Neither one of us is getting much sleep. Would a massage be any help?"

"Probably," said Treasure. "Have him call Lila's for an appointment. I'll see what I can do."

Rose Ann fiddled with a paper clip.

Treasure waited.

"One question. Say Gabe comes for a massage. He'll have to be naked for, uh, how long?"

"Naked? Lands, honey, I don't make no one take off all their clothes. I mean they can, and sometimes for a full body massage they do, but if all I'm doing for Gabe is tending to his shoulder, he'll just need to take off his shirt, is all."

"Really?"

"I don't make Miss Lavada strip down all the way."

"I know. But I thought that was just because . . ." Rose Ann's voice trailed off.

Treasure headed down the hall, shaking her head. So that was the problem. Word was out in Ruby Prairie that one had to get naked to get a massage? If that didn't beat all.

Lands. About the time she was ready to give it all up, business might finally pick up. *Thank You, Lord. Your timing is always just right. I know that, but I do forget. Forgive me for thinking that sometimes, Lord, You have a tendency to run a bit late.*

Jock, along with the three-shopping-days-left-till-

Christmas crowd, cruised the aisles at Wal-Mart. What did a person get for a pair of teenage girls?

He'd already found three presents for baby Molly—a pink ruffled dress; a soft, stuffed, terry cloth cat; and a battery-operated crib toy that made ten different kinds of animal sounds.

Jock pushed his cart down the aisle. Which way was juniors? He moved past electronics. Maybe he'd get the girls a CD.

"Help you, sir?" asked the middle-aged man behind the camera counter.

"You have digitals?" asked Jock. He hadn't planned on buying a camera, but with Molly leaving in a few weeks and Charlotte's old Kodak on the fritz . . .

The man smiled at the pile of pink baby stuff in Jock's cart. "New dad," he said knowingly. "You're taking a ton of pictures, and the cost of developing is eating you up. I know just what you need." He pointed to a midpriced model camera.

"Say," he continued, "stills are great, but have you considered a camcorder? You'll want one for capturing those first steps, first teeth, first date. They grow up before you know it. Look here. Got a great display model on sale."

Jock's voice caught. "I'm not going to be needing—" He stopped. Why not? Did it matter that Molly was leaving in a month or less? They still needed pictures. Something to remember her by.

A scene from the future grazed his mind. He and Charlotte were at home in a darkened room, sitting in front of the TV, watching footage of Molly over and over again. Once she was gone it would be all they would have. Suddenly buying the camcorder became something he had to do.

"You're right. I do need both," Jock told the man. "Fix me up. Any accessories I need?"

After electronics, Jock looked at his watch. Thirty minutes before he was supposed to meet Grady for lunch. Still no gifts for the girls. With such long lines at the checkout, he'd best get a move on.

House shoes, maybe? They had some shaped like yellow ducks. He wished he'd thought to ask Charlotte about Maggie's and Beth's sizes. On the end of the aisle was a display of nail care kits. Girls liked to do their nails. He unzipped one of the cases to look at the tools inside. What exactly did a person do with an orange stick?

Around the corner was a display of music boxes. Was that something a young girl would like? Then again, maybe jewelry would be a better gift. Did either of them have pierced ears?

In the end, Jock bought the girls two gifts each, embroidered denim purses and enormous collections of makeup all packaged together in sparkly, lime green plastic cases. He hoped Maggie and Beth would like them, but he saved the receipts just in case.

For Treasure and Jasper, Kerilynn and Catfish, he picked out extra-fancy Whitman's Sampler boxes of chocolates. And for Kirby, a handheld video game.

. . .

"Sorry I'm late. You been waiting long?" Jock greeted Grady in the foyer at IHOP.

"Less than ten. Looking good, man." Grady slapped Jock on the back.

"Hungry?"

"Am I. Smelling all that good grease. My stomach's been rumbling since I walked in."

Over coffee, while they waited for steaks and fried eggs, Jock showed Grady the ring.

"Wow. It's a beauty," said Grady. "When did this all come about?"

"Well, it hasn't exactly." Jock put the ring case back into his pocket. "I mean, I haven't asked her yet."

"But she knows you're going to." Grady stirred sugar into his mug.

"No."

Grady added cream.

"Charlotte's had a lot going on. Nikki and Vikki, the first girls she took in, left just the other day. She's been pretty busy getting ready for Christmas. We've not exactly been able to spend a lot of time together."

"She still have the baby?"

"Yes. But not for much longer. Parental rights will be terminated soon. Then Molly will be available for adoption."

"Do they know who'll get her?"

"There're lots of couples out there waiting on a baby. I imagine they've got one lined up."

"And you plan to spring a proposal on Charlotte. When?"

"Christmas night."

"You expect her to say yes."

Under the table, Jock cracked his knuckles one by one. "I love her, Grady. I believe she loves me. She's the kindest, most compassionate person I've ever met. I've spent way too much time thinking about our relationship. It's time to do something about it."

"You realize you'll be taking on not just a wife, but a houseful of girls," said Grady.

"I know what I'm getting into. There's some kind of drama going on with those girls every day, but I love them. I believe in what Charlotte's doing. It'll take some getting used to, but I think I could live pretty happily with that bunch of women."

The waitress brought them their eggs. "More coffee, sir?"

"I propose a toast," said Grady, raising his topped-off mug when she'd gone. "To you. To Charlotte. May she say yes."

Jock's mug met his.

"From your lips to God's ears, my friend."

Chapter Seventeen

O f all days for the oven to go out.
Charlotte stood in front of the cold steel contraption and wondered what to do next. It was not yet seven, but she could hear someone stirring upstairs. Molly reclined in her little seat in the middle of the counter where she could keep Charlotte company while she cooked.

Charlotte had planned cinnamon toast and hot chocolate for Christmas morning breakfast. No oven? Oatmeal then. With raisins and brown sugar. The girls liked that. But she'd better let Treasure and Kerilynn know about the oven. Her hand was on the phone when she heard knocking.

"Ho, ho, ho!" Jock's scrubbed but still sleep-creased face appeared through the glass panes at the kitchen door. He held a plastic laundry basket piled high with wrapped presents.

Charlotte cinched up her robe and swung the door open. Mavis and Jasmine barked at her feet. Snowball and Visa meowed for fresh food.

"You're up early, Santa. Merry Christmas. My goodness, what have you brought?"

"Only a few things for the good girls who live in this house. You want these under the tree?" He wiped his feet on the mat.

"Hi, Pastor. You bring any presents for me?" Maggie skipped into the kitchen.

"Have you been good?"

"Very, very good. I've been more good than anybody else in this house."

Charlotte winked at Jock as he headed for the living room. He sure did smell good. She wiped at the spit-up on her shoulder.

Jock placed his piles of presents under the tree. "Ouch." A crispy needle poked him in the ear.

"I sort of forgot to keep it watered," said Charlotte.

"Where's Molly?" he asked.

"Goodness. I left her sitting on the kitchen counter."

"I'm starving," said Maggie. "Beth's still asleep. You want me to wake her up?"

Jock went to get the baby.

"I'm awake. What's for breakfast?" Beth came down the stairs and plopped down on the sofa next to the tree.

"I was going to make toast in the oven, but it won't go on. Which means I need to call Treasure—" Just then Charlotte looked out the picture window behind the tree. Treasure, Jasper, and Kirby were coming up the walk. In the street behind them, Catfish and Keri-lynn were just getting out of Kerilynn's station wagon.

"Did you flush?" Maggie asked Beth.

"What? Of course. Why're you asking me that?"

"No reason. Just I forgot to tell anybody that I think the upstairs toilet might be stopped up."

No oven. Clogged plumbing. Merry Christmas to all.

Charlotte had had the perfect day planned. She'd told everybody to come about nine. A holiday CD would be playing softly in the background. She was going to have a fire blazing, and the scent of her new cranberry-scented candles would greet everyone when they came in. She'd be wearing her new snowflake sweater, perfume, and even a touch of lip gloss.

Seven fifteen. House full of guests.

And here she was—still in her gown.

Heading upstairs with a plunger.

Moving Christmas to Jock's place was his idea. While way smaller than Tanglewood, his compact Craftsman-style house did have a working oven and a toilet that flushed. While Charlotte showered and the girls had their oatmeal and juice, the others packed everything up.

Jock went on ahead to hastily prepare for the change in holiday venue. He tossed dirty socks into the hamper, placed his breakfast dishes into the dishwasher, bagged up overflowing trash cans, and sprayed down the bathroom with Formula 409. There wasn't time to do more. He was just lighting a fire in the fireplace when the front door opened.

"Where's your Christmas tree, Pastor?" asked Keri-lynn after all of them had filed in.

"Don't have one. Sorry."

Except for the one Christmas he was married, he'd

never had a tree. What was the point? During the holidays, he got invited to other people's homes several nights a week. If there was a need to entertain, he took folks out to dinner at Joe's or 'Round the Clock. If he did put up a tree, nobody would see it but him. Other than the perky poinsettia on the hearth, sent to him by Grady and his wife, his house was pretty much devoid of holiday ornamentation.

"No tree," whined Maggie. "Where we gonna put the presents?"

"Maggie," hissed Charlotte. "Be nice. It's Christmas."

"This is a fine house, Pastor," said Treasure.

"Good of you to have us over here," said Kerilynn. "Tree or no tree, we're going to have us a wonderful day. Sugar," she said to Jasper, "let's get all this food into the kitchen. Some of it's going to need more than just a warming up."

"Let's pile the presents on this bench till we get ready to open," said Jock. He cleared newspapers, mail, books, and odd pieces of clothing from the antique church pew in his entryway.

Everybody gathered in the living room, except for Treasure and Kerilynn, who were making themselves at home in the kitchen.

"Need help finding anything?" asked Jock.

"Nah. We're fine," said Kerilynn. "Don't you know a woman can walk into a stranger's kitchen and locate something a man can't for the life of him find in his own house?"

172

"You go on back in there." Treasure shooed him away.

Jock went to the radio in the living room. Some nice holiday tunes would be a good way to set the mood. This was, after all, a holy day.

"Grandma Got Run Over by a Reindeer" immediately filled the room.

"I wanna open presents now," said Maggie.

"Not till after we have our Christmas dinner," said Charlotte. She was seated in a worn leather armchair next to the hearth, Molly in her lap.

"And have our naps." Catfish winked at Jock.

"Naps. Right. Everybody's got to take a long nap after dinner," said Jock. "*Then* we'll open gifts." He feigned a yawn. "I'm pretty tired. Guess we'll all take really *lo-o-ong* naps."

"Looks like our baby here has already started on hers."

"She's sleeping away her first Christmas," said Charlotte.

"Lots more ahead of her," said Catfish.

Jock stood at Charlotte's side, looking down at Molly. She was so beautiful. Whoever got this baby would certainly be blessed. He thought about Christmases to come. Molly at one year. Three. Six. And ten. A little girl with a mom and a dad. Her adoptive parents would be the ones putting together Molly's first bike, filling her stocking with sweets, taking photos for the family Christmas card.

Enough about the future. That was surely all ahead.

173

Good stuff. But today, on Molly's first Christmas, she was here in his house.

Which was a very big deal.

This was the perfect time to pull out his new camera.

"Y'all need help in there?" Charlotte called to the kitchen crew.

"No, ma'am. We're fine," Treasure called back. "You just keep ever'body entertained in there while we get this meal together."

"That fire ain't putting out much warmth," said Catfish. "You sure you're burning seasoned wood?"

Jasper got up to give the embers a stir.

Kirby, Beth, and Maggie sat on straight chairs across from Charlotte. All three were wearing blank expressions, not talking to each other or to any of the adults in the room.

"What's the matter with you kids?" said Catfish. "Y'all look like your best dog up and died on you. It's Christmas."

"I'm bored," said Maggie.

"There's nothing to do," said Kirby.

"I'm tired," said Beth.

Jock went to the hall closet and brought back an assortment of board games.

"Monopoly," said Kirby.

"Pictionary," said Maggie at the same time.

"I like Scrabble," said Beth.

Pictionary it was.

"Back in my day, kids didn't have time to get bored," Catfish began. "We had too much to do.

Chores. I was working a full-time job by the time I was fourteen."

Kerilynn came in with a platter of cut-up fruit and marshmallow fluff dip. She popped her brother on the arm as she walked by. "Don't listen to him. I'd hardly call a paper route a full-time job."

The girls giggled. Kirby grinned.

Catfish shot his sister a look. "It was a long route. Had to get up at four."

"Seven," Kerilynn countered. "Don't believe him when he says he walked barefoot uphill in the snow to school both ways either. Y'all want a little snack? Dinner'll be ready about one."

As the smells from the kitchen grew stronger— turkey, corn-bread dressing, praline-topped sweet potatoes, green bean casserole, and homemade yeast rolls—Jock's anxiety intensified. Unbidden, his hand kept slipping into the pocket of his loose-fitting jeans to feel the box that held the diamond ring.

Still there.

And yes, *still* there.

Moving the celebration to his house had put a kink in his plans. He'd intended to stay late at Tanglewood, under the ruse of helping clean up. He'd pictured himself and Charlotte, alone in front of the fire in a quiet house, at the foot of the lit Christmas tree. They would be sipping hot chocolate, reflecting upon the day. Molly would be asleep in her crib, and he would get down on one knee, ask Charlotte to marry him, and she would say yes.

Okay.

No problem.

He'd come up with Plan B.

Christmas dinner was the best he'd ever had. Keri-lynn had made something called pumpkin roll for dessert. Treasure had brought pecan pies. Jock ate so much that, in fact, once the meal was over, all he really did want was a nap. From the looks on the other adults' satiated faces, they felt the same.

But not the teens.

"Presents! Presents!"

Even Kirby, who in Beth's presence tended to be subdued, joined the girls in their campaign to open up gifts.

And what gifts.

From Kerilynn, Avon cologne for everyone, even baby Molly.

From Treasure and Jasper, sweatshirts and socks for the adults, DVDs for the teens, and a pair of footed sleepers for Molly.

Charlotte presented everyone with books. Teen novels for the kids, a board book for Molly, cook-books for Kerilynn and Treasure, a book on gardening for Jasper, a true crime exposé for Catfish, and for Jock, a leather-bound blank book so he'd have a place to record his thoughts.

From Catfish? Oh, my. Pocket-sized copies of the United States constitution and tiny American flag lapel pins. Even Molly got one of her own.

"Never forget," Catfish said, as he passed out his

gifts with tears in his eyes, "brave young men have laid down their lives for what you got holding right there in your hands."

"No women?" asked Maggie.

"Shhh," whispered Charlotte.

"Pastor Jock. You get us anything?" asked Maggie, when enough reverent time had passed.

"Sure did," said Jock. "Saved the best for last."

Catfish blew his nose.

The girls loved their presents. Kirby too. Treasure and Jasper, Catfish and Kerilynn opened up their boxes of candy right then and started talking about which ones they liked best.

Food consumed and gifts opened, a lull settled over the room.

"What a good Christmas we've all had," said Treasure.

"The Lord has blessed us," said Jasper. He gave his wife's hand a squeeze.

"Say that again. We're lucky to be alive in the land of the free," said Catfish.

Jock got up and put another log on the fire. Even after he sat back down, everyone's eyes stayed on the flames. The room got quiet, except for the sounds of the fire cracking and popping. "Silent Night" played on the radio.

"Pastor Jock," Maggie broke the silence. "You didn't get anything for Charlotte. What about her?"

"Um, I did," stammered Jock. "But it's not ready yet. I have to give it to her later. Sorry."

"You didn't need to get me a thing," assured Charlotte. She put Molly up on her shoulder and patted her back for a burp.

It was an awkward moment. One that lasted too long. Finally Jock reached for his Bible. "Today has been great. Good food. Fun. Everybody being together has made it a great holiday."

"Sure has," murmured the adults.

"I've had fun," said Beth.

"Let's remember the greatest gift of all. The one God sent."

And everyone stayed quiet as Jock opened up his Bible to read to them from the gospel of Luke.

Chapter Eighteen

What do you mean, you didn't ask her?" It was Grady on the other end of the phone.

Jock sat on the side of his bed in his underwear. He had slept in. The ring box sat on his dresser, right next to his keys, wallet, and a roll of Certs with only one left. Any more time in his pocket, and the velvet box would begin to look like something he'd picked up at Goodwill. He rubbed his temple.

"Long story. It got crazy yesterday. Nothing worked out like I planned. I don't know. It just didn't happen."

"So what now?"

"New Year's. I'm taking her out. Planning on asking her then."

"A whole 'nother week," said Grady. "You sure you're not crawfishing on this?"

"'Course not."

"Okay then. Call me as soon as you've got something to report, my friend."

Charlotte tried not to let her feelings be hurt. She'd spent time picking out Jock's gift—granted it was time online—but still, those were some late nights spent searching for just what she'd had in mind. She thought the leather-bound journal perfect. That he hadn't gotten her anything stung.

Which was way childish.

She chided herself. It had been a lovely Christmas Day. Good food, good friends. What more could anyone ask for on a holiday? She tried not to be a person who put value on material things.

Still, it was the thought, or rather Jock's lack of it, that bothered her.

Maggie would have given anything to be with her mom over the holidays. And Charlotte felt bad for her that she didn't even get to visit, but truthfully, having Maggie and Beth at Tanglewood during the holidays had made the day so special. Treasure and Kerilynn had cooked enough food that she had leftovers frozen for several more meals. And Catfish had sure added a colorful touch to the day. That man! No doubt he'd expect them all to be wearing their flag pins on Sunday.

She swiped at Molly's little bird mouth with a soft cloth. Actually, Molly was the one who had made it a holiday Charlotte would not forget. She hoped Jock had gotten some good pictures. He'd taken dozens, been all over the place with that video camera. Maggie had loved it. Beth and Kirby too.

She kissed Molly's cheek.

Six weeks.

That's how much longer Kim expected Molly to be at Tanglewood. Termination of rights was coming up soon.

Then adoption.

By some deserving couple.

And Molly would have exactly what she needed.

Kerilynn had asked Charlotte yesterday if she planned to attend the adoption proceedings. She wasn't sure. It would be a time of joy for one family. A day of indescribable loss for her. And for Jock too.

How would she get through it? One would think God would make doing the right thing easier. That He would somehow take away the pain when a person was doing something pure and good. Why couldn't He provide some sort of holy anesthesia?

If it's all the same with You, Lord, I'll just sleep through it. Wake me up when all this is over.

Charlotte fingered Molly's tiny rosebud toe and thought about Jesus' birth. How in the world did God see fit to send His son in the form of a baby—so vulnerable, so dependent upon the kindness of others? Even more befuddling—how did He manage to give

180

Him up to die on a cross for a bunch of mostly ungrateful folks?

I suppose, Lord, that You do understand my pain. I wish knowing that made it easier. It should. But it doesn't. Please, please, just give me the strength.

She thumbed through the mail. Nikki and Vikki's grandmother had sent a Christmas card. Inside was a picture of the two of them and their mother. They wore grins wider than the teeth on a comb. If anything made the pain of giving them up worthwhile, it was that picture. She'd have to frame it and put in a place where she'd see it every day.

Someday she'd likely receive a picture of Molly and her new family. They would be young. The mother would be pretty and the daddy would be tall. They'd smile for the camera, squinting in the sun that would inevitably be shining. Molly would be dressed in something new. They'd have a dog, probably a grinning yellow lab. There would be a tidy brick house in the background with a swing set already up, waiting for the day Molly would be big enough to play.

Charlotte scooped the baby from her tabletop seat up into her arms. She cradled Molly's soft head in her hands and looked into the little girl's sleepy eyes.

Please, God. Help me to be glad. Because that's not at all how I feel.

New Year's Eve.

The first day of the rest of his soon-to-be-engaged life.

181

At least that's what Jock hoped. What he'd prayed for. What he'd thought of day and night since figuring it all out. He was on the steps of Tanglewood before he realized he'd forgotten the ring.

"Hey, Pastor Jock." Maggie swung open the door before he could turn around and go back. "Come on in. Charlotte's not ready yet. She told me to watch for you."

Jock stepped inside the brightly lit entryway, then into the adjacent cozy living room. He pried Snowball from her favorite spot so he could sit down on one of the sofas in front of the fireplace.

Maggie plopped down beside him and got right to the point. "Happy New Year. You and Charlotte going to kiss at midnight? That's what you're supposed to do."

Jock hadn't thought of that. A first kiss on New Year's Eve was not a bad idea. Nor was it one he cared to discuss with a hormone-fueled fifteen-year-old.

"So," he said. "You and Beth going to the 'Round the Clock party?"

"Yep," said Maggie. "All the youth from Lighted Way are going. Kerilynn says she's not open for anybody but us kids. We're gonna play games and watch some videos and eat and stuff. Charlotte said you guys would drop me and Beth off. Molly's already over at Treasure's house."

Beth came down the steps. "Happy New Year, Pastor."

Then Charlotte, from her bedroom downstairs,

stepped into the room. She was wearing a dress, deep blue, kind of drapy. And pretty silver earrings. Silver shoes too. High-heeled sandals. They made dainty clicks when she walked across the hardwood floor.

"Wow," said Maggie. "You look fancy. I never saw you wear that dress before."

"You look very nice," said Jock.

"Where y'all going?" asked Beth.

"I've got reservations at that new place out on the lake."

"There gonna be dancing?" asked Maggie.

"I don't know," said Jock. "Since Charlotte's got on her dancing shoes, I sure hope so."

She was so pretty when she smiled.

"Everybody ready?" asked Charlotte. "Hope you don't mind dropping the girls off."

Of course he didn't.

Finally it was just the two of them in the truck. He put in an instrumental CD.

"That's pretty," said Charlotte.

She smelled like gardenias.

He steered toward home. "Sorry, but I need to run back by my house. Can't remember if I turned off the iron when I finished pressing this shirt. Drive me crazy wondering if I don't stop and check."

"No problem. You better go see."

He parked in his driveway, but left the engine running. "I'll be right back."

Jock sprinted up the steps, fumbled with his key, and opened the door. He knew exactly where he'd set the ring, so he didn't bother to turn on a light. Two steps into the hallway, his feet touched the edge of the oriental rug.

Squish. Squish.

What the—?

He flipped on a lamp.

No.

Water. Everywhere. Coming from the bathroom, running down the center hallway toward the front door, seeping sideways into both of the house's two bedrooms, edging toward the kitchen and the living room too.

He waded down the hall to the bathroom, where water—clean, thank the Lord—poured over the sides of the toilet. He'd flushed it just before he left, and apparently the bowl had filled . . . and filled . . . and kept filling. First the bowl, then the bathroom floor, now his whole house.

What a mess. He'd only been gone half an hour. What if he hadn't had to come back for the ring?

The ring.

Charlotte.

At a time like this, not being a man given to cursing put Jock at a distinct disadvantage. What was he supposed to do now? With this awful mess to clean up, the romantic evening he had planned was a total bust. There would be no romantic dinner. No dancing.

For sure no midnight kiss.

Lord, are You trying to tell me something that I don't want to know?

184

It took four hours, two shop vacs, three volunteer firemen, and the help of a pair of Lighted Way deacons to get the soggy mess cleaned up.

"Good thing you don't have wall-to-wall carpet," said Gabe.

"Ain't doing much good for these hardwood floors," said Catfish. "They's all gonna have to be refinished."

Charlotte, who at the sight of the wet situation had changed out of her dress and into a pair of Jock's cinched-at-the-waist sweatpants and one of his old shirts, passed glasses of iced tea and Coca-Cola to the living room full of sweaty, tired men, then sank onto the sofa.

"You don't know how I appreciate this," said Jock.

"All in a day's work," said Gabe, the volunteer fire chief. "Honey, you got any sugar to go in this tea?"

Jock motioned for Charlotte to stay put. He got up and fetched the sugar.

And was she ever glad. She yawned. What a night. All she wanted to do was go home and crawl into bed. As for tomorrow, she'd be so sore she wouldn't be able to move. It was nearly eleven. The girls' party was over at one. Molly was spending the night at Treasure and Jasper's.

Maybe they'd all sleep in tomorrow.

The men finished their drinks, then got up to leave.

Jock walked them out and stood on the porch till they were gone. Charlotte didn't move from her spot. Honestly, she wasn't sure she could. How many buckets of water had she mopped up? Ten? Twelve? Her arms ached, and she had blisters on both thumbs. She leaned back in the chair and closed her eyes.

"Charlotte?" Jock's face was close to hers.

She rubbed her eyes and moved to sit up straighter. What was this? She must have drifted off.

Jock's house, brightly lit during all the cleanup, was now dim. A trio of chunky candles flickered on the coffee table. Next to the candles were a bottle of sparkling grape juice and two stemmed glasses. He had changed into a clean shirt. Put on cologne too.

"Goodness. Did your electricity go off too?" Charlotte motioned toward the candles.

Jock laughed. "Thankfully, no. We didn't get to have our big date, so I thought I'd at least try to make it a little bit festive in here. It's nearly midnight. Almost the new year."

"It looks nice."

"Tonight didn't turn out anything like I'd planned."

She shot him a grin. "What do you mean? I've always dreamed of spending New Year's Eve with a half-dozen men. It was ta-ru-ly special. A night I'll remember forever."

Jock didn't smile. Instead, he studied his knuckles. "I hope that's the truth."

Charlotte shivered.

"You're cold," said Jock. He snagged an afghan off the back of a rocker and brought it to cover her legs. Then he sat down next to her, close enough that their

186

knees touched whenever either of them shifted on the worn, cushy sofa.

"I got sweaty mopping," said Charlotte. "Guess now I'm chilled."

"How about a toast?" said Jock. He poured them each a glass of juice.

"To the new year," said Charlotte.

"To all that it holds," said Jock. His smile appeared strained.

Charlotte sipped.

Jock gulped.

He set his glass down.

Charlotte held on to hers. She looked Jock in the eye, but he was scanning the floor.

"Something you need to talk about?" she asked. Folks confided in Jock all the time. She wanted to be the kind of friend he could share his heart with, a person he could trust.

"There is." His moist eyes now met hers.

Molly. That was probably it. Charlotte didn't say anything—just reached over and took his cold hand in hers.

"You know my past," said Jock. His thumb stroked the back of her hand. "After my divorce, I believed I was meant to be alone. Felt that was the way I could best serve God. I didn't want to take the chance of ever hurting someone the way I hurt my wife back then."

"You were nineteen," said Charlotte. "And God's long ago forgiven you. You're a different person than you were back then."

Jock nodded. "My head knows that. My heart has been a bit slower to believe. I've avoided getting involved with anyone out of fear that it wasn't the right thing. But lately I've gotten to the point where I'm ready to move on, to look forward instead of backward."

"That's good," said Charlotte. She sneaked a glance at the clock on the wall. Nearly twelve. Soon she'd need to head out to get the girls. "You deserve to live your best life today."

"I'm glad you agree," said Jock. He took a deep breath. "Because I know with all my heart that my best life includes you. I didn't expect it. I didn't look for it, but, Charlotte, I'm in love with you. I want to be your husband. I want to be with you for the rest of my life."

Charlotte's hand went to her mouth.

"Please," said Jock, "let's don't wait. Time's never going to stand still. Real life gets in the way. I want us to be together. The sooner the better. Please tell me that's what you want too."

Charlotte put her hand on Jock's arm. "Jock," she whispered. "You are the most unselfish person I know. That you would do this for me means more to me than you'll ever know. It is the kindest offer I've ever heard anyone make. But it's not a good reason to get married. It just isn't."

"What are you talking about?"

"Molly. Offering to marry me so that I can keep Molly, so that she'll have the two-parent family she needs." She wiped at tears with the back of her hand. "It's a sweet and generous thing you're offering, Jock. But it would be wrong. For so many reasons. It would just not be right."

Chapter Nineteen

Jock sat stunned. He'd hoped for a yes, realized he could get a no, had reluctantly considered that Charlotte might stall for time before giving him an answer. But never, ever had he entertained the possibility that this woman he loved with all his heart would so misunderstand his motives.

The clock over the mantel struck twelve.

"Charlotte." He swallowed. "You're wrong. This isn't about Molly. It's about how much I want to be with you. Even if Molly hadn't come along, I'd still be asking you, tonight, to marry me. Do I love Molly? Of course. It's killing me to think of her leaving. But my feelings for you have nothing to do with her."

Charlotte's voice was soft. "You're not being honest with yourself, Jock. Your emotions for me are all tied up with Molly. My feelings for you are tangled up with her too. I think it's impossible to separate them. Neither of us is thinking straight."

"Listen to me." Jock took both her hands in his. "I'm thinking perfectly straight. Molly's adoption is already in the works; you told me so yourself. You think I would even consider crushing the hopes of some young couple who think they're about to get the child of their dreams? To pull Molly back from them would be cruel. Our getting married won't change anything about Molly's future. It never crossed my mind that it would."

Charlotte's eyes widened. "So this . . . really isn't about figuring out a way to keep Molly?"

"Oh, Charlotte." Jock shook his head. "Not at all."

Charlotte looked at the floor. For a long moment neither of them spoke.

Finally Jock lifted Charlotte's chin with his hand. "Answer one question. Do you love me?"

"Yes." Charlotte began to weep. "I have for the longest time."

"Do you want to be with me?"

She wiped at her eyes. "Every minute of every day. That was one of the best things about Molly coming into my life. You were always around."

Jock grinned. "What can I say? She was a great excuse to show up at Tanglewood unannounced. Somebody had to make sure you two were doing okay."

"If we—if we get—um—together," Charlotte stammered, "what about Tanglewood? Can you handle living in a houseful of women?"

"I believe I can," said Jock. "If we, as you put it, 'get together,' our lives will forever be in a fishbowl. Our business will be the church's business. I'm on call to the meandering Lighted Way flock twenty-four hours a day. Think you can you handle that kind of a life?"

"I believe I can," said Charlotte.

"So, are you saying yes?" Jock's voice cracked. "Are you saying you'll marry me?"

"Pastor," said Charlotte, all done with tears, "I do believe I am."

"Just like that?" said Treasure. "You and the pastor are getting married? Honey, I can't believe it."

Charlotte sat at Treasure's kitchen table with Molly in her arms. Fully awake at seven, she'd left the girls sleeping off their New Year's Eve fun to come get the baby.

Treasure reached toward the sparkly jewel on Charlotte's hand. "Let me see your ring." The diamond sparkled under the light.

"That's gorgeous. Why, that little sneak. He had this all planned." Treasure shook her head. "I can't wrap my brain around it. Shoot. Ever'body in town's known you two were perfect for each other since forever, but when nothing seemed to be happening, we all but give up. Girl, we've got some big plans to make. Gon' be a real celebration. You set the date?"

"We have."

Treasure got up to pull the calendar off the kitchen wall and set it on the table between them. She turned forward several months. "Tell me when, so I can mark it down right now. You know the whole town will turn out for you and Jock on your big day." She dug in the kitchen drawer for a pen and a pad.

"Let's see. There's the flowers and the cake and the music. Your dress. You're not wearing white, are you? I know lots of second-time brides do, but I've always thought it didn't seem quite right. 'Course, it's your wedding, dear; don't let me rain on your parade."

Charlotte let her friend run on.

"Ain't one thing wrong with it, if you've got your heart set on white." Treasure stopped to take a breath. "Okay, baby, I'm ready. Tell me the date."

"Friday," Charlotte said. She raised her mug for a sip. "We're getting married this coming Friday. Seven o'clock. At Lighted Way."

Monday morning, Jock and Charlotte were enjoying a blissful morning all to themselves. It was a two-hour drive to Kim Beeson's office, and Jock didn't mind the trip one bit. They'd take care of business, have a nice lunch, and enjoy the ride back to Ruby Prairie.

Since the news of their engagement broke, the two of them had barely spent a minute alone. According to Kerilynn, reactions at 'Round the Clock were mostly good. Only a few Ruby Prairie folks thought the speed of their impending nuptials a bit scandalous. Grady had been thrilled when Jock called to tell him Charlotte had said yes and ask if he'd perform the ceremony. Beth and Maggie, while shocked at first, were excited about the wedding, especially when Charlotte told them they would get to be bridesmaids.

Getting the paperwork and background check done

so that Jock could move into Tanglewood was the one hitch in their speedy wedding plans. Long as they got right on it, Kim had told them she didn't think it would be a problem, though with four days left before the wedding, they were cutting it a bit close.

"Congratulations," said Kim. She motioned for them to take a seat in mismatched chairs across from her cluttered desk. "I'm so excited for the two of you. Jock, you'll be such an asset to Tanglewood. It will be wonderful for the girls to have a father figure in the home. Not many of them have ever had that in their lives."

"I hope I'll be good at this," said Jock. "I've not exactly had lots of experience being a father."

"There's training you'll need to complete within the next few months. I'll get you information about all that," said Kim. "For now, let's get these forms signed. These two you need to fill out front and back. This other one you just need to sign to authorize a background check. Standard for anyone involved in the care of children. What about your test for TB?"

"Got it this morning," said Jock, holding up his arm. "Nurse at the clinic said she'd fax the results to you when she reads it day after tomorrow."

"Good," said Kim. "If there's anything else I need, I'll give you a call. Looks like things are in order."

"Can you come to the wedding?" asked Charlotte.

"Wouldn't miss it," said Kim. "How're Maggie and Beth taking the news?"

"Good," said Jock. "They seem excited. Of course,

193

Beth leaves to go back to school two days after the wedding, so this doesn't affect her so much."

"You know Maggie's going to try you and test you," said Kim.

Charlotte and Jock both smiled and nodded. They knew.

"I have some news about Sharita," said Kim.

"Is she okay?" asked Charlotte. "I'm sorry she'll miss the wedding, but she won't be back from winter break."

"Sharita's more than okay," said Kim. "Her parents are moving out of their old neighborhood into an area that's much safer . . . in Nebraska."

"Nebraska?" Charlotte looked stunned. "Are you telling me . . . Sharita's not coming back to Tanglewood?"

Jock reached for her hand.

Kim nodded. "I'm sorry you didn't have a chance to say good-bye. You'll need to box up her things and ship them UPS. I've got the address for you right here."

Charlotte didn't cry, but Jock felt her hand grow cold and damp. Tears would come later.

"Are you okay?" Kim focused on Charlotte.

"No," said Charlotte. "But I will be." She swallowed and squeezed Jock's hand.

Jock wasn't sure Charlotte could hold it together much longer. He was ready for this meeting to be over.

"I have something else to discuss," said Kim.

Great.

"Charlotte, you've told me it was important to you that Molly be adopted by a two-parent family."

Jock couldn't believe this woman. Bringing Molly up right now, just after telling them about Sharita not coming back, was like twisting the knife. Couldn't she see Charlotte was barely holding it together as it was?

"That's what every child deserves," said Charlotte.

"Well, since you're getting married, have you considered adopting her?" asked Kim.

"We would never do that to another couple," Jock said. "To take Molly away from a family who's expecting to get her would be wrong."

Kim looked at him like he'd gone nuts. "What family? What are you talking about?"

"You told me Molly's adoption was in the works," said Charlotte.

"It is."

"So there's a family expecting to get her," said Jock.

"No-o," said Kim. "I don't know who told you that. We don't match a child with a family until termination of rights is completed. Too much can go wrong."

For a moment no one spoke. Then, "So . . . there is no family?" asked Charlotte.

"Lots of families wanting to adopt, but no one specific yet," said Kim.

"So this means that we could . . ." Jock's voice trailed off.

"Molly could . . . ," whispered Charlotte.

"If you decide you want to adopt Molly, the two of you would be considered first, since she's been with

Charlotte since the beginning. I can say almost with certainty that, assuming termination of parental rights goes through, Molly would be awarded to you."

"Treasure?" Charlotte, unable to wait to share the awesome news, made the call on her cell phone before they'd even gotten out of the parking lot. "You're not going to believe this. We've just had the best news ever."

Jock reached over and gave her a kiss on the cheek.

"It's about Molly." Charlotte was laughing and crying all at the same time. "Jock and I are going to adopt her. . . . Yes! . . . No. They didn't have a family for her yet. She's going to be ours. Really. She's going to be my daughter—I mean, our daughter. Oh, can you believe it? . . . Soon. Really soon. They have to get termination of parental rights. It'll be right after that. Oh, Treasure. Isn't God just so, so good."

Chapter Twenty

"Miss Lavada," said Treasure, "you're all packed up. Going home today, I hear."

"No, honey, nothing wrong with my ear," said Miss Lavada. Using a cane, she was moving around her little room steady as could be. "I'm going back to my house today. Doctor's released me. Says I'm going to be fine."

Treasure spoke up a bit louder. "That's wonderful. I'm so glad. Your kids picking you up?"

"No. Not going to need a truck. All I've got is my clothes. A few books. Some little knickknacks. You want this little stuffed cat? Some children came and left it on my bed. I don't have any use for it."

Treasure gave her a hug.

Miss Lavada pressed a sack of Hershey's Kisses into her hands and patted her cheek. "These are for you. You've been so sweet to me. I can't thank you enough for helping me get back on my feet."

"You're welcome, Miss Lavada. You're welcome as can be."

"See you at church on Sunday?"

"Yes, ma'am," said Treasure. "I'll be there. You want me and Jasper to pick you up?"

"No. I already told you. There's no need for a truck. Remember, dear? I live right next door to the church. I'll walk over, just like I always do."

With Charlotte and Jock's Friday night nuptials less than forty-eight hours away, wedding plans were proceeding at a dizzying pace. Lighted Way ladies, called to action by Treasure, Kerilynn, and Ginger, converged in the fellowship hall to assign last-minute tasks.

"Can't believe those two were not planning on having any flowers," said Treasure. "Ginger—you're fixing her a bouquet and Jock a boutonniere, right?"

"Me and Lester are picking them up at Sam's Club," said Ginger. "Jennifer, the floral manager, does a real good job over there. What y'all think about pink roses and baby's breath?"

Treasure marked flowers off her list. "Sounds real pretty. Ever'body know to keep track of your expenses? We'll divvy it all up even when everything's said and done."

"Gabe's taking pictures," said Rose Ann. "Got a new digital camera. He told Jock he'd be the official wedding photographer."

"Nomie and I've got the cake ordered, and we're doing up raspberry sherbet and ginger ale," said Sassy Clyde. "Makes a pretty punch."

"Lila's going over to Tanglewood to fix Charlotte's hair," said Kerilynn.

"Doing Maggie and Beth as well," said Treasure. "Upsweeps, she said."

"Charlotte get herself a new dress?" asked Ginger.

"Gone to that new little shop over in Ella Louise after one today," said Treasure. "She was planning on wearing one of her regular church dresses. I told her not every day a woman gets married. She owed herself something new." She looked at her watch. "Sorry, girls, but I've got to get down to the shop. Got two clients back-to-back."

"You think you could work me in later on today?" asked Nomie. "I been meaning to call, but I never can remember."

"Half hour or whole?" asked Treasure. "If you just want a half, I could do you about three."

Charlotte and Jock sat hand in hand on Tanglewood's front porch, both in short sleeves. It was past midnight. Inside, Molly, Maggie, and Beth slept. The street in front of Tanglewood was still and quiet, lit by a clear white winter moon, undisturbed by even a hint of breeze.

"Texas weather," said Charlotte. "I'm still not used to it. Thirty-five one day, seventy-two the next. In January."

"Unless a cold front comes through," said Jock, "we may have to turn the air conditioner on in the church tomorrow night. Building'll be packed. Don't want anybody passing out during our vows."

Charlotte smiled. "That would make for some memories." She ran her finger along a vein in the back of Jock's hand.

Jock kept the porch swing in motion with his foot—back and forth. The chains above their heads creaked and groaned with every sway.

Charlotte could feel the warmth of his shoulder and arm against her own. They'd kissed. Tentatively, cautiously, the first couple of times. Then, so perfectly, so deliciously, it was like they'd known each other's lips for all of their lives.

Amazing how quickly one's kissing could improve.

"Penny for your thoughts," said Jock.

Charlotte studied her engagement ring. Some

thoughts she'd wait to share.

"Just can't believe the way everything's worked out," she finally said. "You. Me. Molly. This time tomorrow night, we'll be husband and wife. Imagine. A week ago, we weren't even engaged."

"Way I see it," Jock teased, "when you're our age, you don't have that much time to waste."

Charlotte smiled. "You saying we're old? Maybe instead of the honeymoon cabin at the lake, we should book a couple of connecting rooms at New Energy."

"Uh, we're not that old," said Jock. He shot her a suggestive grin. "You're sure you're all right with just two nights away? That's a pretty short honeymoon. Grady said he'd stay and preach if I needed him to."

"Of course." It had been her idea that they drive in from their honeymoon destination, an hour away, on Sunday morning in time for Jock to preach. "Since Lighted Way's where everything started, I can't think of a better place for us to begin the first week of the rest of our lives. Besides, what's this about only two days? I thought the honeymoon was supposed to last forever."

He sure hoped that it would.

Jock stood at the back of the empty sanctuary. Eight hours ago, he'd told Charlotte good night. About ten hours from how, she'd come down this very aisle to marry him.

He'd be down at the front.

Wearing a new navy suit.

Waiting for her.

God, I believe I've been waiting for her all of my life. Thank You. Oh, thank You so much for this day.

The weather was gorgeous. Supposed to be in the high seventies by noon. Texas weather. The cabin he'd rented for the weekend faced the lake and had a wide deck that extended out over the water. This time tomorrow, he and Charlotte could be basking in the sun. Or they could be out in the boat doing a little fishing. Or they could be taking a hike.

Jock sat down on a back pew intending to pray. His thoughts wandered. One never knew. It could rain the whole weekend. This time tomorrow he and his new wife could be holed up inside that little cabin by the lake.

And wouldn't that be one big crying shame.

Thank You, Lord was as far as Jock could manage to get. Hard to pray a formal prayer when a smile keeps threatening to split your face.

He figured God understood.

In her nightgown, Charlotte moved from the kitchen toward the staircase to go up and wake the girls. Kerilynn was bringing over breakfast. Ginger had already called about the flowers. Lila planned to fix the girls' hair early and do hers right after lunch.

The photo of her late husband, J.D., on the wall of the stairwell stopped her. She lifted the picture off its hook, held it in two hands, and slowly sat down on the third carpeted step. She pulled the tail of her gown

201

over her bare feet and pulled her knees to her chest.

J.D. had been gone for nearly three years. What a good man he'd been. The husband of her youth. Twenty years they'd spent growing up together. They'd expected to grow old together.

She touched the frame with her hand. Wiped dust from the glass. Then a tear from her eye. Finally she stood up and carefully placed the photo back on the wall, eased it to the right so that it hung straight. It would need to come down. Others too. She would put pictures of Jock in their places. Of her. Of baby Molly. She'd put the ones of J.D. in a nice album.

But not just yet.

The ladies surveyed their work.

"Looks lovely," said Ginger. "The perfect setting for a country wedding."

"I think they'll be pleased," said Treasure.

"I hope so, 'cause I have worked up a sweat," said Kerilynn. She pulled a dish towel from her tote bag and wiped her face.

Lighted Way's sanctuary had been cleaned and polished from one end to the other. The scent of lemon oil wafted from every pew. Two big baskets of roses and carnations adorned each side of the space where Charlotte and Jock would stand to take their vows, under an English-ivy-adorned arch borrowed from Miss Lavada's side yard. All this was where the communion table usually stood.

"Hope Lester didn't hurt himself too bad," said

Nomie: "I never would have guessed the communion table was that heavy."

"He'll be all right," said Ginger.

"If he's not, have him come see me at the shop on Monday," said Treasure.

"I always wondered," said Kerilynn. "You make the men take off their pants when they get a massage?"

"I don't *make* them do anything," said Treasure. "But no matter what I do, I keep them draped. I respect their modesty. Why you asking?"

"No reason," said Kerilynn. "Just wondered. Business is picking up, looks like."

"I'll soon be as busy as I want to be," said Treasure.

"You sure did wonders for Miss Lavada," said Ginger. "Bless that poor old woman's heart. So glad she's back in her house."

"Those candles look nice," said Sassy rather abruptly.

Treasure knew for a fact that Sassy still believed massage therapy to be rather suspect.

"Same ones we used for the Thanksgiving service," said Kerilynn. "Ones Catfish made out of all those tuna cans. He just rigged 'em so as we could stand them up inside." She looked at her watch. "Ladies, if we're going to make it to this wedding, we best get ourselves home and get cleaned up. Ever'thing's set for the reception, right?"

"All done," said Sassy. "Cake's ready to be cut. Nuts and mints are already out. Got plenty of cups and plates. Just have to stir up the punch. Can't do that till they've said their I dos."

• • •

"Is it true it's bad luck for the bride and groom to see each other on their wedding day?" asked Beth.

"My cousin says it is," said Maggie.

"No such thing as luck," said Gabe Eden. "Now you two girls stand right there in front of the fireplace so I can get your picture."

"What about Molly?" said Maggie.

"Can you hold her?" asked Gabe. "Be nice if we get all three of you pretty girls together."

Unseen, Charlotte watched them from the entry hall. The girls looked lovely. All three wore outfits in shades of pink; Maggie a bright orange-and-pink floral dress that set off her carrot-colored curls, Beth a medium rosy pink sweater over a floaty pink skirt, and Molly a white crocheted dress with a touch of baby pink trim.

"I never been a bridesmaid before," said Maggie. "What we got to do?"

"Just walk down the aisle and give everybody one of your beautiful smiles," Charlotte said, coming into the room.

She was thrilled to have the girls be a part of the ceremony. They would stand up beside her, Beth holding Molly. Jock's choice of best man had been tough. He'd not wanted to hurt anyone's feelings. In the end he'd asked Jasper, who, according to Jock, had teared up.

"You look beautiful, Charlotte," said Gabe. "Pastor's gonna drop his teeth when he sees you. Let's get a shot of you with the girls, then some of you by yourself on the staircase. Too bad it gets dark so early this time of year. Some pictures outside would be nice."

Charlotte had looked to buy herself a pink dress too, but at the tiny shop in Ella Louise, she'd fallen in love with a simple, soft green, tea-length gown. Cap-sleeved with a princess neckline framing her late mother's tiny gold locket, the dress fit snugly in the bodice, then skimmed her hips to end in a gentle flair.

Even she had to admit that Lila had done an incredible job with her hair. With a curling iron Lila had softened Charlotte's natural, slightly frizzy curls, then piled them on top of her head. Loose tendrils framed her face. A few escaped curls wisped at her neck. Mascara set off her blue eyes. Rosy pink lipstick framed her smile.

"How come you're not wearing a big white wedding dress?" said Maggie. "You know. The kind with the thing that goes over your face."

"A veil? Because this is my second wedding," said Charlotte. "Most people only wear white the first time."

"Did you have a white dress the other time?" asked Maggie.

"I did."

Beth shot Maggie a look.

"It's okay," said Charlotte. "I've been thinking about my first wedding today too."

Gabe coughed and began to fiddle with the settings on his camera.

"That was a happy day. This one is too. There's room for lots of really happy days in every person's life." She gathered the girls into her arms. "I'm happiest of all that you three girls are here with me now. Gabe? If we're done with pictures, I think we'd better get going. I'm getting married in half an hour."

When Jock and Grady pulled up at Lighted Way twenty minutes before the ceremony should commence, Jock knew at once that something was wrong. Half the townspeople, dressed in wedding finery, were standing out on the church lawn, close to the street. The side door as well as the double doors at the back stood open. Looked like every light in the building was blazing.

Catfish was at Jock's passenger side window before he could even get out. Lester, shaking his head, followed close behind.

"Got a problem, Pastor," said Catfish. "Don't believe you'll be getting married here tonight."

Not again. Antique plumbing. In every house and business all over town. Would it never end?

"What is it this time?" asked Jock. "The baptistery? One of the sinks? Please tell me it's not a backed-up toilet." He pushed his way through the crowd to see how bad the damage was.

"Jock, wait," said Lester.

"Pastor, I wouldn't," warned Catfish.

"It ain't what you're thinking," said Gabe.

Jock kept going, determined to see what could possibly be wrong. Water? Could be cleaned up. Broken sound system? No problem. Grady'd just have to speak up loud. There was no glitch he could think of that would get in the way of the most important event of his life.

At least that's what he thought until he bounded up the front church steps, only to skid in the foyer like a Saturday morning cartoon character. His eyes watered. His nose ran. He retreated faster than a lazy man from a hoe.

Surely among the smallest of God's furry creatures, yet the one packing a most powerful punch, the skunk was no longer present in the church. But it had left its unmistakable, lingering mark.

Chapter Twenty-one

I've done called the exterminator people," said Cat-fish. "They've got some stuff they said they could spray. S'posed to help, but they won't be here for a couple more hours, and I don't know how much good they can do tonight. Pastor, what you want to do about the wedding? Put it off?"

"No. Not putting it off." Jock could feel himself beginning to sweat. "Anybody seen Charlotte? Is she here?"

"Her and the girls are across the street at Miss

Lavada's. Kerilynn got hold of them soon as they drove up," said Lester.

The parking lot and the streets on both sides of the church were beginning to fill up with cars. Folks meandered around under the streetlights, all of them wanting to know what Jock was going to do.

"Couldn't we just move the wedding to one of the other churches in town?" asked Grady.

"First Baptist has got their revival going on. Expecting lots of folks from out of town. Neither the Methodist nor the Assembly of God is big enough to hold this crowd," said Jock.

Grady thought for a moment. "How about we have it out here?" He motioned toward the tree-bordered side yard of the church. "All we'll need to do is move the volleyball net and set up some chairs. Nice flat spot. Moon's full. Sky's clear. Weather's nice. It'll be perfect."

And it was.

Soon as word passed through the crowd that the wedding was going to take place outside, Ruby Prairie folks sprang into action. Jock stood like a rooted shepherd and watched the beehive-like activity of his flock go on around him.

Chairs were hauled out from the fellowship hall to the lawn, bucket-brigade style, so folks who couldn't stand for long would have a place to sit. Gabe retrieved a biohazard mask from his EMS bag. Catfish strapped it on and braved the stinky sanctuary to haul out his tuna can sconces. Once they'd been hosed off, he and Lester pushed them into the ground and lit the candles placed inside.

Thankfully, the bride and groom's flowers were still in the refrigerator in the fellowship hall. Treasure pinned Jock's boutonniere onto his lapel, then took the bouquet across the street to where Charlotte and the girls were waiting.

Grady stood at the end of the makeshift, candlelit aisle and called for the wedding guests' attention. "Please. Let's gather around. We've got things in place. Got a groom. Bride's on her way. What more does one need for a wedding? I say we're ready to start."

Old folks, women with children, and pregnant ladies took seats under the canopy of pine trees. Others stood around to the sides. A few retrieved folding lawn chairs from their car trunks and set them up.

Jock and Jasper moved to their places next to Grady. When Grady gave the nod, a trio of Lighted Way girls, accompanied by a boy on a guitar, began to sing a medley of soft praise and worship songs. As the music floated upward, mingling with smoke from the candles, the noisy crowd shushed one another and grew quiet.

"You ready?" Treasure asked Charlotte. She handed over the clutch of pink roses tied with white satin ribbon.

"Yes," said Charlotte, trembling only a little. She

and the girls stood ready and waiting in Miss Lavada's tiny living room.

"No doubts?"

"Not one."

Treasure gave Charlotte a kiss. "You four look so pretty. Everything's ready." She wiped a tear. "I still can't believe you and the pastor are finally getting together. Sugar, I've been praying about this for so long."

"So you're the one responsible." Charlotte smiled.

"Me and the Lord."

"When are we going?" asked Maggie. "It looks like they're waiting for us." Since they'd begun their vigil in Miss Lavada's house, she'd taken on the task of peeking through the living room mini-blinds, announcing to Charlotte and Beth details of the activity taking place across the street.

"Hey. Something happened. The streetlights just went out."

"Gabe told me they was going to shut them off when they were ready for you to come out," said Treasure. "Going to be a candle and moonlight wedding. 'Sides, those big lights attract too many bugs. Guess they're ready. Charlotte, honey, are you?"

Oh, yes.

She was ready.

The full white moon was so bright that once the street-lights had been dimmed, it cast long, lacy, tree-filtered shadows onto the street in front of the church. From

210

his spot next to Grady and Jasper, Jock did not move his eyes from their focus on Miss Lavada's front door. When at last he saw it open, then close, then open again to reveal first Maggie, then Beth carrying a sleeping Molly, and finally Charlotte, he exhaled, not even aware he'd been holding his breath.

Slowly they came down Miss Lavada's front sidewalk, crossed the street, stepped onto the grass, and moved up the candlelit aisle. At the front, the girls stepped to the side, but Charlotte moved directly to him. In the moonlight her skin was pale, her eyes bright, her hair golden and soft against her face.

Jock took both her hands in his.

Grady addressed the crowd. "To everything there is a season. A time and purpose for every matter under heaven. We gather this night to celebrate the marriage of Jock and Charlotte. Do you who love them offer your blessing on this union?"

"We do!" responded the crowd.

"Amen," said someone a little bit late.

Grady smiled. "Then let us begin." He turned his attention to Charlotte and Jock.

"We come to celebrate the gift of your love, something holy, sacred, and rare. May the two of you always remember this night and the meaning of the vows you are about to take. Repeat after me. . . ."

"I, Charlotte . . ." She spoke clearly, without even a quiver. ". . . Take you, Jock, to be my friend, my husband, my companion for the rest of my life. I promise to walk with you through whatever troubles and sorrow life may bring. I vow we will journey together, sharing all the goodness, joy, and light God showers on us. With these words, as well as the unspoken words of my heart, I offer myself to you. I bind my life to yours in marriage, for as long as we both shall live."

Jock began in a strong voice, gazing directly into Charlotte's eyes. "I, Jock, take you, Charlotte, to be my wife, my companion for the rest of my life." He paused, coughed, and swallowed twice.

"Take your time," said Grady.

"I promise . . ." Jock's voice cracked. ". . . To walk with you through . . ." He wiped at a tear. ". . . Whatever troubles and sorrow life may bring."

At this point Jock, embarrassed and overcome, had to stop. When he let go of Charlotte's hands to wipe his face with his sleeve, she took him in her arms and began to dry his tears with her handkerchief.

"I'm sorry," he said, choking the words out. "I love you so much."

"It's all right, darling. I love you too," she said, as if no one else existed in the world.

The crowd remained still.

Finally Grady put his hand on Jock's shoulder and said, "Whenever you're ready, we'll start back up."

Jock nodded and stood up tall. With Charlotte glued to his side, word by word, he spoke his vows.

When he was done, Grady prayed, then again addressed the relieved and sympathetic crowd. "By the power vested in me as a minister of the gospel of Jesus Christ and by the state of Texas, I ask that you as witnesses join me in pronouncing Charlotte and Jock—" He raised his hands.

"Husband and wife!" the crowd proclaimed with one voice.

"Mr. and Mrs. Masters," said Grady, "now you may kiss."

Jock leaned down toward Charlotte, paused, then leaned down a bit more. At the very moment their lips touched, *BANG! POP! CABOOM!*

Charlotte and Jock jumped.

Molly woke up and began to cry.

"Fireworks," explained Grady in a loud whisper. "Fifty dollars' worth. Kids saved 'em from New Year's. They were going to set them off as you left the church. Guess they decided not to wait."

"Wow," said Jock. He took Molly from Beth, arranged her against his shoulder, and stroked her little back, which settled her right down. His free arm circled Charlotte's waist. "Would you look at that," he said.

Roman candles, bottle rockets, sparklers too.

Charlotte leaned against him. For a moment the three of them, along with their wedding guests, remained motionless, engrossed in the surprise light show. Then Jock, still cradling Molly, bent to plant a thorough, not-to-be-interrupted kiss on Charlotte's lips.

"Ahh," sighed the crowd, then burst into applause at the sight of their romantic silhouette outlined in fiery starbursts against the night sky.

Chapter Twenty-two

Pastor's wife.

Her newly acquired title, printed in the day's order of worship, made Charlotte smile. She sat in the third pew from the front with Molly on her lap. Beth sat on her right, Maggie on her left. The girls, who after the wedding stayed at Tanglewood in the care of Treasure, had rushed into her arms as soon as they'd tumbled out of the van at Lighted Way, behaving as if she'd been gone for a month instead of a day and a half. Neither wanted to sit with friends as they did on other Sundays. This morning they needed to squeeze in right next to her.

Charlotte understood.

Change.

It was difficult for all of them, and lots more was coming down the pike. This afternoon Jock would move his clothing and personal things into her down-stairs bedroom at Tanglewood. Over time, they'd sort out what furniture of both of theirs they'd keep, what would be stored, and what would be given away.

On Thursday, she and Jock would drive Beth to the airport, put her on a plane, and send her back to Colorado to school. Charlotte would miss her, but again she thanked God for Beth's opportunity. It had given her a fresh start.

In just over two weeks, Maggie would return to her mother. According to Kim, she had gotten back on track while incarcerated. She'd passed her GED, taken parenting classes, and participated in job training. She and Maggie were moving into a rent-subsidized apartment, and there was every reason to be optimistic about their future.

Reunification. Always the goal.

Charlotte had repeated the phrase to herself over and over these past couple of months. Not only was Maggie leaving, but also Donna was not coming back. Once she'd gone home for the holidays, her dad decided not to send her back to Tanglewood. Charlotte had talked to her on the phone, barely waiting until she'd hung up to cry.

Due in part to Grady's wise counsel, she and Jock had decided to put a hold on any more Tanglewood arrivals for now. "Take six months. Enjoy each other," he'd advised. "You and Molly need to get used to being a family of three. Give yourself time to settle into your new routines."

Kim had understood. She would place no more children at Tanglewood until Charlotte and Jock gave her the word. They would be in prayer, believing they would know when the time was right.

The cabin had been wonderful. They'd enjoyed every minute of their day-and-a-half honeymoon.

215

Even if it had rained nonstop.

On Sunday morning they drove back to town and went directly to Lighted Way, arriving early enough to unlock the doors and turn on the lights. The sanctuary still carried the slight smell of skunk, but thanks to the fumigation efforts of the company Catfish called in, the smell was tolerable.

Once inside the building, Jock's focus was on the morning's service. Charlotte took a seat on the back pew and watched her new husband move around the sanctuary, checking the microphones, the communion trays, the neat stack of church bulletins at the back. She watched as he went briefly into the restrooms, both ladies' and men's.

"Toilet paper," he explained. "Sometimes they forget to put new rolls out."

Finally, he looked at his watch, eased down beside her, bowed, and asked God to bless the congregation who would gather on this day.

It was after one o'clock before Jock, Charlotte, and the girls got home from church. Their appearance at the Sunday morning service brought from the congregation endless hugs, many good wishes, and a few sly winks.

Once the last person exited the building, Jock locked up and suggested that the five of them splurge on a pasta lunch at Joe's. Charlotte thought it a great idea. So did the girls.

Once they were seated and served, Maggie and Beth

chattered nonstop. Charlotte balanced Molly on her knees while Jock hurriedly downed his meal; then he took over so that she could eat. In honor of their marriage, Joe himself served them complimentary cheesecake and coffee for dessert.

Charlotte left feeling content and stuffed. She went to put Molly down for her nap as Maggie and Beth climbed the stairs to change out of church clothes. Jock plopped down on a sofa in the living room, loosened his tie, flipped on the TV, and picked up the Sunday paper.

At the sink in the bathroom, Charlotte looked at her reflection and marveled at how right it all felt. She and Jock. Married. How normal and comfortable and wonderful, and yet how strange!

Thank You, God, for this good day.

It was when she went into the kitchen in search of a Tums that Charlotte saw the blinking light on the answering machine. Most likely someone peddling magazine subscriptions or vacation condo rentals. Those people had to make a living, but they sure did call a lot. She pushed Play, then reached into the fridge for a bottle of water.

The machine gave its shrill beep; then the message began. "Charlotte? Jock? You there? Mark Lister here, at the police station on Sunday morning. Got a little problem. Could you give me a call? Better yet, could the two of you come down here soon as possible? Thanks."

Jock was immediately off the sofa and at the counter

beside her. "What could that be about?"

"I don't know," said Charlotte. She stared at the machine and felt her heart speed up.

"You think it's okay to leave the girls here?"

"Yes. I'll tell Maggie and Beth to come downstairs so they can listen for Molly in case she wakes up. She'll probably sleep for a good two hours. They can call us on the cell if they need us."

"It's probably nothing," said Jock. "Some little something with a Lighted Way member or one of their crazy relatives. Or maybe they've arrested a drunk who's requested to see a minister. I get all kinds of calls, day and night."

Charlotte stared straight ahead. "But Mark asked for both of us."

"Did you forget? You're now the pastor's wife," said Jock. "Didn't take long for folks to figure out we're a two-for-the-price-of-one deal. Well, no point in guessing. We'll find out soon enough."

When they entered the waiting area at the station, the receptionist picked up the phone and called Mark to come up.

In just a minute, he came through the security door to lead them to his office. "Y'all come on back. Take a seat. Coffee? Soda?"

"We're good," said Jock. "What's up?"

"Baby at home?" asked Mark.

What an odd question.

"Yes. She's with Maggie and Beth," said Charlotte.

"And she's doing all right?"

218

"Fine. Of course. She's fine," said Charlotte. "We left her taking a nap."

Enough with the chitchat. Why were they here?

"And y'all have had her, uh, the baby, for how long now?" asked Mark. He was looking at the calendar on his desk.

"Since just before Thanksgiving," said Jock.

"Have you adopted her?"

"No. Not yet. Judge has to terminate parental rights. That's set for this week," said Jock. He leaned forward in his chair. "What's all this about?"

"Don't know how to say this." Mark fiddled with a paper clip. Bent it. Bent it again. Broke it in two.

"What?" asked Charlotte. She wanted to choke the words out of his mouth. Having lost her parents in a car wreck when she was eighteen, a baby to miscarriage when she was thirty-seven, and her husband to cancer not three years ago, she knew what people looked like when they were about to deliver bad news.

Mark stood up. He walked to the window, pulled a hanky from his pocket, and wiped at his mouth. "Young woman came into the station just before noon. Been waiting to talk to y'all. Said she'd wait no matter how long it took you to get here."

"Who is she?" asked Jock.

"What does she want?" asked Charlotte.

"The baby," said Mark. "She wants the baby. Claims she's the mother."

Chapter Twenty-three

Treasure couldn't shake the feeling of something being wrong. She went down the hall to peek in on Kirby. He was asleep in his room, mouth wide open, snoring like an old man. Jasper? She could look out her kitchen window over the sink of soaking soapy dishes and see him putting out feed for the horses.

She went to the front window, stood looking out at the road that ran in front of their house. *Lord, my spirit's troubled. Don't know why. You do.*

The Holy Spirit often prompted her to pray. Times past she might have ignored it, mistaken that uneasy feeling in her gut for indigestion. Not now. Having reached her midsixties, Treasure had learned to pay attention.

Lord. Take care of whoever it is that's in need. Step in. Take care of Your children, whoever they be.

She didn't hear Jasper come in and jumped when he came up behind her and wrapped his arms beneath her ample chest and planted a kiss on her neck.

"What you looking at out there?" he asked.

"Nothing really," she said, leaning back against him. "You care if I drive over to Tanglewood?"

"'Course not. What's going on?"

"Nothing I know of," she said. "Probably silly, but I

can't shake the feeling I might be needed. I'll just pop in and make sure everything's okay. Don't look to be gone long."

In tandem, Charlotte's and Jock's chins dropped.

"Could be a hoax," said Mark. "But I don't think so. Take it slow. I'll bring her in. Y'all talk."

Charlotte's mind reeled. This could not be. Molly was two months old. Her abandonment had been in all the papers. The police had searched for her parents. No one had come forward. She and Jock were married now. They were Molly's parents. Hadn't God worked it all out perfectly? Of course He had.

She breathed in. This was a test of faith. One she was ready for. God would not let Molly be taken away. Not a chance.

"This is all some big mistake," said Jock. His face had gone red, and he spoke through his teeth. "We aren't letting some stranger come in and take Molly. She's ours. The adoption is in the works. It's been approved." He couldn't stop. "Somebody left her like an animal on the floor of my church. Charlotte's been taking care of her. No way—whoever this woman says she might be—is she going to march into our lives and claim that baby now."

Mark sat back down. He took off his glasses, rubbed at the spot between his eyes, then put them back on. "I understand. This is a shock. I feel for you, I really do. But before you say anything else, you have to hear this woman's story."

Charlotte reached for Jock's cold hand. She swallowed down the acid bile that rose in her throat. Faith. She had to have faith. And she needed a Tums. Everything was going to be all right. She squeezed Jock's hand. Managed to stretch her dry lips into a smile. There was no need to be worried.

Bless this poor woman's heart. How desperate she must be try to pull something like this. Wonder where she was from and how she'd heard about Molly. "What–what's her name? This woman. The woman who's claiming she's Molly's mother."

"Emily," said Mark. "Emily Reed."

"How do you know that's even her real name?" blurted Jock.

"She's got ID," said Mark. "Driver's license. She checks out. No criminal record. Comes from Tennessee. Says she and her boyfriend were driving through east Texas when she went into labor. He didn't even know she was pregnant until she gave birth at the motel over in Ella Louise. Next morning, driving down the road, he threatened to hurt the baby if she didn't get rid of it. Says that's why she left her at the church.

"For the past two months she's been trying to get away from him, but the creep wouldn't let her out of his sight. Threatened to kill her if she left him. Finally, a week ago Monday, he got arrested in Florida on a drunk driving charge. If all this checks out, I reckon they'll charge him with kidnapping too.

"Anyway, Miss Reed called her mama to come get

her. Soon as she could get her hands on a car, she drove herself here. Twenty straight hours."

"She can't be legit. You see it in the papers all the time," said Jock. He was talking way too fast. "Women try to kidnap babies when they can't have children of their own. Maybe this Emily person heard about Molly. Thought she could come here and take her."

"I don't believe that's the case," said Mark. He reached for the phone on his desk. "She's been waiting over two hours. I'm calling for her now."

They waited. Jock's knee bounced up and down. No one spoke. Charlotte heard two sets of steps coming down the hall. Now at the door. She and Jock stood up at the same time as if pulled by string.

Emily Reed was young. Perhaps twenty-five. African American, but very light-skinned. Thin. Chin-length brown hair. Tired eyes. Hopeful eyes. Wearing jeans, a tan sweater, sneakers. As soon as she saw her, Charlotte began to cry. Her mind said no. Her heart said yes. Before the girl even spoke, she knew.

This woman was not the enemy. She was not some crazy person with an outlandish claim. She was not someone to be pitied, nor someone to be fought or judged.

She was Molly's mother.

And she was crying too.

Emily's sobbed-choked words tumbled out. "Where is she? Is she all right?" Her eyes flew from Charlotte to Jock, then back to Charlotte again. "Do you have her with you? They said you found her. I was so scared. I didn't know what to do. Thank you for taking care of her. Oh, please, please, let me see her. I've been so worried. Please tell me she's all right. She is all right, isn't she?"

Charlotte willed herself to reach out to Emily, but her feet wouldn't move. She just stood there, looking, listening, breathing in the girl's words, her hands limp at her sides. The room's heater kicked on. She heard the *whoosh*. Felt warm air on her cheek like the gentle brush of a cat.

"She's fine," she whispered, standing very, very still. Was that her voice? Coming not from inside her, but from somewhere way off?

Jock moved his body between hers and Emily's. Only then did Charlotte move—to crumple into his arms like a balloon with no air.

Chapter Twenty-four

B lood tests proved Emily Reed's identity.
Miss Lavada confirmed her story.

Lucid and sharp now that she was back home in her own house and off all of those pain pills, Miss Lavada recognized Emily immediately. Yes. She was the tearful and trembling young woman with the baby who had come to her door looking for the pastor of

Lighted Way Church. Miss Lavada recalled directing the girl to the fellowship hall, explaining that if the pastor wasn't in his office she should check over there.

'Course, it was the very next day she had taken that bad fall. Things were a bit fuzzy for a time after that.

Treasure, when she allowed herself, wondered exactly how glad she should be about the improvement that getting back on her feet had brought about in Miss Lavada's cognition. In her heart, she knew nothing she'd done had changed the course of things.

Still.

What if Miss Lavada hadn't remembered? It would have been hard to prove Emily Reed's story about how she happened to unwillingly leave that baby in the church.

So many *what-ifs*.

So many *whys*.

The biggest question, the one hardest to ask, was where exactly was a loving God in all of this awful mess?

Treasure hated that sometimes the ways of God did not make one bit of human sense.

Take Charlotte and Jock, for instance. People do something that's purely good. Like take in an unwanted child. Love it. Care for it. Give it everything it needs. One would think that doing such a selfless deed would prompt the good Lord to give such people as that some kind of a break. Award them a couple of Get Out of Jail Free cards.

But God didn't always work like that.

From Treasure's vantage point, people like Charlotte and Jock, who chose to lay down everything in service to Him, often saw their lives get harder, not easier. And folks, when faced with such hard things, tended to go one of two ways.

Most every person got mad at first.

That was normal.

But depending on how they were turned, either they stayed mad or they didn't. The people who stayed mad stewed in their disappointment and lived their lives acting as if they'd been betrayed, or at least cheated out of something they were owed.

But the other folks? The ones like dear Charlotte and Jock? Once they were past all that mad, they fell into God's arms, because they really and truly had no place else in the whole world to go.

5:30 a.m.

Maggie was at a friend's house, where she'd spent the night.

Jock slept.

Charlotte could not. She sat on the side of the bed for a long moment before easing her feet to the floor, slipping on a robe, and moving to the nightlight-lit hallway outside their room, where Molly's bassinet was set up.

Even though the baby still dozed, Charlotte lifted her from the bed. Molly stirred a bit but didn't wake up. Charlotte, barefoot, padded into the darkened living room, where she eased down onto the sofa and stretched out on her back, keeping the baby snug against her chest. Molly's downy soft head fit perfectly under the warm crook of her chin. Charlotte loved the baby's scent. She inhaled, exhaled, her breath like a prayer for which there were no words.

The bassinet would come down today. Charlotte was giving it to Emily to take back with her to Tennessee. Not only the bed, but also the car seat and the bathtub and the swing. And of course all of Molly's clothes, toys, and blankets.

Emily would need those things.

Charlotte would not.

Emily arrived just after ten, from Lester and Ginger's house next door. They'd offered her their spare bedroom for the past five days, while Emily got to know her daughter, learned how to care for an infant, and waited for the legal go-ahead to take Molly home.

Charlotte and Jock wanted this handing over of Molly to her mother to be private. Jock asked Kerilynn at the 'Round the Clock to pass the word around Ruby Prairie.

Please. No big send-off.

Not this time.

Lester and Ginger came over with Emily, but they didn't stay. Lester helped Jock pack up Emily's car. Ginger delivered warm sweet rolls, crisp bacon, and fruit, which Charlotte and Jock both said looked good, but which neither of them touched.

• • •

The departure didn't take long.

Few words were said.

The weather had turned cold during the night. Wind from the north. No rain, but clouds obscured the sun. Jock carried Molly out. Emily buckled her into the car seat. He and Charlotte bent and kissed her good-bye. Charlotte closed the car door. Jock pressed two hundred dollars into Emily's hand.

She hugged them. Said thank you.

And then they were gone.

Chapter Twenty-five

Charlotte blamed it on the $500 Home Depot gift certificate given to her and Jock as a wedding present by members of Lighted Way two weeks after their wedding.

Gabe Eden took the pulpit to present them with the generous gift. "Y'all probably figured after all this time we wasn't going to do nothing for you, but we been planning this all along. Just took us awhile to collect. Couple your age isn't needing sheets and towels or pots and pans to set up housekeeping with," Gabe allowed, "but we're proud for y'all just the same. We figured, big ol' house like Tanglewood's always going to need something fixed or replaced.

Y'all save it till you need it, or go on and spend it now. It's yours to do with what you want." Gabe wiped his eyes. "We wish you a long and happy life together."

The congregation rose to applaud, and Lester Collins moved to the microphone to give the closing prayer. But before he could begin, Catfish stood up and motioned for him to wait. Prior to the congregation being dismissed, he needed to remind Charlotte and Jock of their patriotic right and duty to spend that certificate on American-made products.

Folks shuffled in the pews. They had roasts in the oven. Cranky kids who needed naps. Some sneaked looks at their watches. Kickoff was in twenty minutes.

Those near the back gazed longingly at the door. When Catfish got going, it took him awhile to figure out exactly how to get stopped.

Thankfully, this time, when he said what he'd intended to say, then began saying it all again, circling like the pilot of a single-engine plane looking for someplace to land, Kerilynn motioned for him to put on the brakes, come back, and sit down in his pew.

Much to the relief of the congregation, he did.

The rest of February and all of March were filled with activities and responsibilities. Once Maggie was gone, Charlotte threw herself into cleaning and de-cluttering Tanglewood from top to bottom. She and Jock held a garage sale, getting rid of stuff so as to more easily combine their two households.

First of March was the weeklong revival at Lighted

Way, which took up lots of Jock's time.

Charlotte hosted the mid-March meeting of the Ruby Prairie Culture Club. A gardening guest speaker from over in Ella Louise spoke with evangelistic fervor against the widespread practice of severely pruning flowering shrubs. She gravely encouraged club members to Stop Murdering the Myrtles—which turned out to be a controversial topic if ever there was one. Heated discussion was prompted, a good two-thirds of the members remaining stalwart on the side of winter pruning, with the undecided others leaning only slightly toward the side of natural growth.

Ginger tried to end the emotional discussion by announcing to all that refreshments were ready to be served. But it was Botox that saved the day. Over slices of triple-fudge bundt cake, Kerilynn let slip the rumor that Rose Ann Eden, unbeknownst to Gabe, had actually let some quack inject that stuff right into her face. After that announcement, not one of the club ladies gave any more thought to the state of their crepe myrtles.

On their first trip to Home Depot, Charlotte and Jock roamed the aisles like disoriented hikers, over-whelmed by the vast array of shelter-related products available in the store. Who knew there were so many ways a person could fix up a house?

While Charlotte found the concept of making changes to their abode mildly interesting, Jock got bitten by the bug. What started out as a quest for new kitchen countertops morphed into an entire room redo. Plans for new white Corian led to the need for new cabinetry. Which led to a lust for new sinks and appliances. By then, replacement flooring and lighting were the only logical ways to go.

Which was why Charlotte, after Jock left for his office, found herself making coffee and toast in the living room, washing dishes in the bathtub, and keeping the milk and eggs in an ice chest at the foot of their bed.

What a mess. Dust everywhere. Gaping holes where the old appliances had been ripped out. Bare subfloor. According to the contractors Jock hired, it would be at least two weeks before the new kitchen was completely done. Probably more like three.

Charlotte took her coffee to the porch swing.

In contrast to the chaos of the house, Tanglewood's yard looked lovely. What a beautiful spring so far. Green everywhere. Grass. Flowers. Trees. Cool but sunny air. Charlotte swayed back and forth, waved at Ginger across the yard, and stroked Visa, who'd jumped up in her lap.

Thank You, God, for this good day.

Surely no one deserved to be as content as she. Jock was not a perfect husband. Theirs was not a perfect marriage.

But most days he, and it, came awfully close.

Few people asked, but Charlotte knew folks in town wondered how she and Jock were coping with the loss of Molly.

231

Some days were better than others. Keeping busy helped. So did having someone in her life who totally understood how random sights and sounds could trigger instant tears. Emily had promised to keep in touch, but after one letter telling them she and Molly were just fine, they had not heard anything else.

Not long after Molly left, Charlotte was shopping at Rick's and ran into a Lighted Way member she didn't know well—one who came to services only a few times a year.

"Don't you regret taking that baby in," the woman asked, "seeing as how you didn't get to keep her after all?"

When Charlotte told her no, she did not, her challenger exclaimed that *she* could never care for children like that because *she* would just get too attached.

It was all Charlotte could do to keep from smacking the woman in the face with a family sized loaf of honey whole wheat.

Jock was right. Some folks were never, ever going to understand.

The ringing of the phone called Charlotte back inside to the mess. She picked her way through the living room, maneuvering around boxes of dishes and kitchen gear and crates of canned food to get to the phone. "Hello?"

It was Kim. They hadn't spoken in nearly two months. After a few seconds of small talk, Kim spilled the beans. "I know you and Jock planned on taking a break from foster care."

"We do. At least through the summer. We'll probably be ready for new placements when school starts. Late August, I guess. I think we'll be ready by then."

Silence on the other end.

Then, "I've got a problem." Kim's words tumbled out. "A sibling group. Four boys. Two girls. Eight to sixteen. In need of immediate placement. None of my other homes have enough room to take such a large group, and I'd hate to split them up. Any chance you'd consider taking them? Even on a temporary basis?"

Charlotte sat down. She looked at the jumble of housewares that filled her downstairs. "Kim, I don't know. We're doing work on the house."

What would Jock say? They'd agreed that it was wonderful having the house to themselves for the first few months of their marriage. But oh, my. Those poor children. How awful for them to go into separate homes.

Charlotte's mind moved room to room upstairs. She could put two boys in two rooms, the two girls in one. Or maybe each girl could have her own room.

Boys! Oh, my. All those pink-and-yellow print quilts would need to be replaced.

Kim interrupted her thoughts. "Charlotte, I know it's a long shot, but would you consider it? See what Jock says? These kids are at a shelter now. I want to get them out of there as soon as possible."

A shelter. Charlotte's heart broke. Those poor kids.

She would run to the church and talk to Jock right now.

Lord, if this is the right thing to do, then please let him say yes.

Jock sat in the doctor's office waiting room, thumbing through *Ladies' Home Journal* while he waited for Charlotte to get through. Over-the-counter antacids weren't doing the job anymore. She needed a prescription. One of those new stomach wonder drugs they were always showing on TV. He looked at his watch. Nearly eleven.

Charlotte should be about done. They hoped to be back to Tanglewood before noon. Kim was coming with the six kids at three. Neither of them had slept much last night. Aided by a host of Lighted Way members, they had worked until midnight, getting things as cleaned up as possible, ready for today.

The kitchen still was torn up. No way to help that. Thankfully, volunteer church members were scheduled to bring three weeks of hot evening meals. Cereal would do for breakfast. The kids could eat the plate lunch offered at school. Weekends he could grill.

Six kids!

Today felt like Christmas. Kim was Santa Claus, bringing six wrapped gifts. He could hardly wait to see what exactly would be inside. Girls! Boys! What would they look like? What kind of personalities would they have?

Jock looked at his watch again. Dr. Strickland must

have decided to run some tests.

Twenty more minutes passed before Charlotte came out.

Jock stood up to go. "She give you a prescription?"

"Yes."

"Tell you anything special you should be eating or not eating?"

"Sort of," said Charlotte. She slipped on her sweater and swung her bag to her shoulder, then paused at the receptionist's window. "You can go on out to the truck. I'll be right there."

"Wow," said Jock once they were on the road headed back to Ruby Prairie. He reached over and squeezed her hand. "Can you believe that in three hours we're going to have a houseful of kids? The days of it being just you and me are about to be over, babe."

"Uh-huh." Charlotte returned his squeeze.

"We going to make this work?"

"Of course." She unbuckled her seat belt, scooted over to his side, and pointed to a spot up ahead. "There's that roadside park up here on the right. You know. *Our* park. Could we stop? Just for a second?"

"It's after twelve," said Jock. This was not the time. They needed to get back to Tanglewood. Kim could be earlier than she said. No telling how many Lighted Way folks were already camped out on their porch, ready to do whatever needed to be done, wondering where in the world he and Charlotte were when six kids were expected this very afternoon.

"Just for a minute. Please? It's our special place. Today's a special day." She kissed him on the cheek.

Jock braked. Put on his turn signal. When she put it like that, how could he refuse? He parked under the pines, and they got out of the truck. Charlotte took his hand and led him to a concrete bench. It felt cool and a bit damp. Ugh. He'd probably have to change his pants.

"Thanks for stopping," she said. "It's so pretty here."

"You're welcome. And yes. It's very pretty here." He willed himself not to look at his watch.

"Listen to those birds," she said, looking upward at the lacy green branches over their heads.

Birds. Bees. Flowers. Trees. His left knee began to bounce up and down.

"I need to tell you something." She spoke slowly.

"Okay." He tried to make his voice sound as though they had all the time in the world for this sort of romantic chitchat.

"It's not just acid reflux."

His knee stopped its dance. "Something worse?"

"Not exactly. I have to go back for more tests."

"But you're all right."

No answer.

"Tell me, Charlotte. You're okay, right?"

Her mouth began to twitch at the corners.

"What is it?" he demanded. *Please, God. Don't let it be anything bad.*

"You know how we decided we could handle six

kids? Well, what would you think of seven?"

"Seven?" Where had the extra one come in? "Well, I suppose. We might have to put up a set of bunk beds."

Charlotte turned her head to the side. "What if the seventh one was really, really little?"

Jock got it.

"You mean you're . . . ?"

She nodded.

"That's what took you so long at the doctor's office? We're . . . ?"

"Uh-huh."

"But I didn't think you could . . . ?"

"Me either."

"Oh, my goodness! We're having a baby!" Jock stood up. Sat down. Stood up again. "No way! This is amazing. I can't believe it." He pulled her into his arms. "We're having a baby? For real?"

"For real."

"You're okay. Right? I mean, you're healthy. The baby. Everything's okay?"

"I'm at higher risk because of my age, but Dr. Strickland thinks everything's fine."

"When?"

"I'm about two months along."

Jock stepped back to touch her belly. "A baby. Our baby. Yours and mine. I can't believe it. We're going to be parents. Of a child of our own. I never . . . I mean, after Molly, I never thought . . ." His voice choked.

Charlotte was crying too. "Me either."

"I love you so much."

After several long minutes, they moved from the bench toward the truck. Jock opened Charlotte's door, then gave her a long kiss before closing it and getting in on the other side.

"Seven kids," he said, once they were both inside the cab. "Not six. Wait till Ruby Prairie folks hear about this. Can you imagine their reaction when they hear we're expecting a baby of our own?"

Charlotte and Jock pulled into Tanglewood's driveway just in time to see Ginger Collins walking up the sidewalk with a big decorated cake. Sure enough, a crowd of smiling folks waited on the front porch.

Ginger's timing was perfect, Charlotte and Jock agreed.

Today there would be laughter. Maybe some tears.

Bunches of prayers.

And cake all around.